PU

VOLCANIC FURY

Only Sam noticed when wisps of yellow-tinged gas suddenly started to boil out of the second fumarole. It bubbled up from inside the volcano and then churned around faster as it leaked up into the sky.

'Dad,' he began, 'what –'

A roaring sound drowned out his words. Gas shot into the sky and enveloped the helicopter. It lurched violently, throwing Sam forward against his seatbelt . . .

There was a sudden reek of gas. Sam felt his eyes stinging. He tried to hold his breath, but he had to gasp for air and he choked as the stuff got into his mouth and lungs . . .

The helicopter swung away from the slope. The engine spluttered and died. Sam caught a dizzying glimpse of grey rock sliding past, and then the tops of trees rushing to meet them.

'We're going to crash!'

Some other books by Jack Dillon

SURVIVE! EARTHQUAKE ALERT
SURVIVE! HURRICANE HORROR
SURVIVE! FIRE STORM

SURVIVE!

VOLCANIC FURY

Jack Dillon

PUFFIN BOOKS

For Peter

Special thanks to Cherith Baldry and Ian Locke
Additional thanks to Dr David Rothery of the
Open University

PUFFIN BOOKS

Published by the Penguin Group
Penguin Books Ltd, 27 Wrights Lane, London W8 5TZ, England
Penguin Putnam Inc., 375 Hudson Street, New York, New York 10014, USA
Penguin Books Australia Ltd, Ringwood, Victoria, Australia
Penguin Books Canada Ltd, 10 Alcorn Avenue, Toronto, Ontario, Canada M4V 3B2
Penguin Books (NZ) Ltd, Private Bag 102902, NSMC, Auckland, New Zealand

On the World Wide Web at: www.penguin.com

Penguin Books Ltd, Registered Offices: Harmondsworth, Middlesex, England

First published 1999
3

Text copyright © Working Partners Ltd, 1999

All rights reserved

Created by Working Partners Ltd, London W12 7QY

The moral right of the author has been asserted

Typeset in Bembo

Made and printed in England by Clays Ltd, St Ives plc

British Library Cataloguing in Publication Data
A CIP catalogue record for this book is available from the British Library

ISBN 0–141–30443–X

CHAPTER ONE

Sam Carlsen pulled himself up the ladder from the hotel swimming pool and stood shaking water from his short, sand-coloured hair. 'Mum,' he said, 'nobody else in the whole wide world does that!'

His mum pushed her sunglasses up on top of her head. 'Does what?'

'Brings a computer down to the swimming pool!'

Liz Carlsen grinned at him. She was wearing a brightly coloured beach wrap and flip-flop sandals and was sitting in the shade of a beach umbrella at one of the small tables around the hotel pool. Her laptop was on the table in front of her and she was tapping away busily.

'These articles are paying for this trip, young man,' she said. 'And don't you forget it. Here.' She groped in her beach bag and held out her purse. 'Go to the bar and get me another drink, will you – orange juice, lots of ice? And one for yourself.'

Sam wrapped a towel round his waist, took the purse and set off round the edge of the pool to the bar. His mum was a travel journalist and his father a freelance photographer. Their work took them to all kinds of exotic locations, like this South Sea island. All Sam's friends thought he was really lucky to go with them, but Sam wasn't so sure.

His mum and dad didn't usually go away at the same time, but they were working together on this particular assignment, and they had brought Sam along as his school holidays had just started. The trouble was, work took up such a lot of their time that it didn't leave much for Sam. He couldn't help thinking about the fun he could be having with his friends if he had stayed at home.

The pool was curved, its contents shining

blue in the morning sun. Bright sunbeds and beach umbrellas surrounded it. Scarlet and purple trumpet flowers scrambled over the low white wall that surrounded the pool area. The place was a tropical paradise, just as the tourist brochures said.

So why do I feel bored? Sam wondered. He wished he had some of his friends here to share it with.

Sam gave his order at the bar and squinted back across the water while he waited for the barman to fetch the drinks. This early in the morning, not many people were about. On one of the sunbeds nearby a girl was stretched out. Even though she was face down, Sam recognized the long, dark hair. He thought back to meeting her at the barbecue the night before. Her name was Jo, and she looked about his own age – fifteen – but she didn't seem to have much on her mind except her suntan. A real airhead, Sam thought.

He had met her younger brother Mike at the same time: a skinny kid with ears that stuck out and a serious expression. Now he was swimming earnestly across the width of the pool at the shallow end.

Just as the barman produced the drinks, Sam saw his father come running down the steps from the hotel. Sam sighed. Russ Carlsen ran everywhere; just looking at him made Sam feel exhausted.

'Hi,' he said to Sam, signalling to the barman for another drink. 'Listen, I've fixed up a helicopter to go and take some pictures from the air. Do you want to come?'

'Yes, sure.' Sam brightened up; this was better than lazing around the pool. 'What pictures?'

'Fumaroles.'

'Fumaroles?' Sam began. 'What are —'

Russ swept on without paying attention to Sam's question. 'I've heard there are some pretty good ones on a little island just north of here. I should be able to get some really spectacular pictures. Let's tell your mum.'

He strode off along the side of the pool, leaving Sam to follow with the drinks. By the time Sam reached his mum's table, Russ was sitting astride one of the chairs, his arms folded on the back, talking rapidly.

'No, I can't.' Liz managed eventually to get a word in edgeways. 'Honestly. If this article isn't finished and e-mailed by tonight, I'm dead. You and Sam go.'

Sam set the drinks tray down. 'Dad,' he repeated patiently, 'what are fumaroles?'

Russ blinked at him. 'Fumaroles? Holes in the side of a volcano. They let out steam and gas and stuff. This island we're going to, Tangaroa, is just about all volcano.'

'Wow! Is there any chance it'll erupt?' asked Sam.

'No, not a hope,' said Russ. 'It hasn't erupted for . . . hundreds, if not thousands of years. I checked it out.'

Sam sucked up his orange juice and let the icy liquid trickle down his throat. If Tangaroa did erupt, he thought, his dad would be delighted. He could just see him, hovering over it in his helicopter, taking pictures. They would be good pictures, too. It was almost a pity he would have to make do with steam escaping from these fumaroles.

'I tell you what,' his dad went on. 'The helicopter has space for four passengers. Let's ask your friends if they'd like to come along.' He sprang up and bounded away along the poolside.

Sam started up, but his dad was already calling, 'Jo! Hey, Jo!'

Sam sat down again. 'They're not my friends,' he said. 'They're no fun.'

'They might be OK when you get to know them,' his mum said.

Sam grunted and watched as Jo sat up and his father stood over her, talking and gesturing. Mike swam to the side of the pool and held on to the side, listening. A minute later he climbed out and both he and Jo disappeared towards the hotel – to ask their parents, Sam supposed.

He fought with feelings of disappointment. He would have enjoyed the trip much more if he'd been with just his dad. Sometimes he felt that he and Russ never spent any real time together. Maybe his dad wasn't interested in him at all. 'He never listens to me,' he said.

'Or me,' his mum said. 'Oh, come on, cheer up. I bet by the time you get back here, all three of you will be good friends.'

Sam finished his drink, draining the last drops of juice from among the ice cubes. 'Suppose so,' he muttered. 'Should I take anything? Some food?'

'No, don't worry about it. You'll only be gone a couple of hours. I'll see you back in the hotel for lunch.'

'Sam!' His dad was calling from the other end of the pool. 'Come on, put some clothes on! The pilot will be waiting!'

Sam got up and forced himself to grin at his mum. 'Yeah, it'll be OK,' he said. 'If that Jo's a real pain, I'll drop her down a fumarole. See you.'

When he paused at the top of the steps and looked back, Liz already had her head bent over her laptop again.

The helicopter was waiting at a small private airfield, about half an hour's drive down the coast road. The pilot introduced himself as Zack. Sam thought he was a local man; he was small and slightly built, with dark hair, though he spoke good English with an American accent.

'I hear Tangaroa looks real good right now,' he said as he led the party across the airstrip to the helicopter.

'Oh, why is that?' asked Russ.

'Some new holes have opened up,' the pilot explained. 'And it's pouring out a whole lot more gas.'

'Does that mean anything?' Mike asked nervously.

'No.' Zack laughed, showing a flash of white teeth in his tanned face. 'Things change over there all the time. Nothing ever happens. Old Tangaroa, I reckon he's been asleep for a long, long time.'

'Tangaroa was a Polynesian fire-god, right?' Sam's dad said.

'Right. Pretty good name for a volcano, huh?'

They reached the helicopter. Russ hoisted up the heavy bag that contained his photographic gear, and climbed in after it. Mike followed, with Jo after him and Sam bringing up the rear.

'This is great,' Mike said excitedly. 'You are lucky, Sam. Our mum and dad like to stay at the beach all day.'

Sam shrugged. 'I guess it's OK.'

Mike slid into the seat next to Russ and started to ask him about his equipment. Sam found himself sitting next to Jo. She flicked her long hair back and gave him a friendly smile.

'I've never been in a helicopter before,'

she said to Sam. 'It's cool!'

He grinned suddenly, excitement rising in him as the pilot climbed into his seat and cut in the engine. He'd only been up in a helicopter once before, but he remembered how much he'd enjoyed it. 'Yeah, it is pretty cool, isn't it?'

The rotor blades began to turn and the helicopter lifted into the air. The last of Sam's boredom dropped away from him just as the ground below did. He peered down as the helicopter gained height and flew over the hotels that fronted the beach, and then headed out to sea. He could see a few sailing boats and a magnificent white yacht that was heading for the harbour, all of them looking very small against the blue water.

'. . . rock so hot it's liquid, right down in the centre of the earth.' Sam started to listen to what his dad was telling Mike. 'It's called magma. Sometimes the pressure underground builds up so much that something has to give in. The magma and gases shoot upwards and that's when the volcano erupts.'

'I'm glad we don't get them at home,' Mike said.

'This is the best part of the world for

volcanoes,' said Russ. 'All around the Pacific, they call it the Ring of Fire. Even so, eruptions don't happen often,' he added reassuringly.

Mike started to ask more questions, but before long he was interrupted when the pilot pointed and said, 'There's Tangaroa.'

At first the island was a dark shape on the horizon, a cone rising smoothly out of the sea. Russ had already started taking pictures.

As they drew closer, Sam could make out more details. The lower slopes of the mountain stretched out like the paws of an enormous animal. They were covered with trees and undergrowth, green and lush, with the occasional splash of bright colour from tropical flowers.

At the foot of the slopes was a strip of beach, edged with a line of foam where the waves washed in. For a minute Sam couldn't think what was odd about it until Jo exclaimed, 'Sam, look! Black sand!'

'That's really weird,' said Sam.

'Mr Carlsen, is the sand black because of the volcano?' Jo asked.

'That's right.' Russ didn't look at her; he was peering through the viewfinder. 'Sand is ground-up rock, volcanic rock is black, so – black sand.'

'I wonder what it would be like to swim off there,' said Jo. 'I've never seen anything like it!'

While they were talking, Zack had been heading for the cone of the volcano, at the eastern end of the island. It rose, grey and sinister, from the surrounding greenery. It was not as smooth as it had looked from a distance. In some places the rock had fallen away into sheer precipices, while in others it looked like rope, as if a giant had taken it up in handfuls and twisted it. Here and there plumes of smoke rose into the sky or drifted gently across the rock face.

Jo shuddered. 'Awesome!' she said.

'Can you take us in a bit closer?' Russ asked.

'Sure,' Zack said.

The helicopter dipped and skimmed low across the summit of the volcano. The very tip of the cone was sheared off, and as they flew over it Sam could see that inside was a vast bowl, sloping gently down to a small lake in the centre.

'Great!' said Russ. 'Hold it right there.'

Zack kept the helicopter hovering above the lake. It looked very peaceful, reflecting the blue of the sky. Sam found it hard to imagine rock and lava shooting out of the crater; the last eruption must have been a very long time ago.

When Russ had finished, the helicopter flew on, over the slopes at the far side. Looking down, Sam could see they were getting closer to a crack in the rock; this must be one of the fumaroles they had come to see. Smoke was billowing sluggishly out of it. The crack was edged with yellow crystals, brilliantly coloured against the grey rock.

'What are those?' Mike asked, pointing.

'Sulphur,' Russ explained. 'There'll be sulphur in the gases that are coming out. Not very nice if you get too close. Smells like rotten eggs!'

The pilot dipped closer, avoiding the plume of gases, but bringing the helicopter only a few metres above the crack in the ground. Just below, Sam noticed, was another fumarole, with barely a wisp of gas escaping.

His dad was muttering away happily,

swapping lenses and clicking the camera from as many angles as he could manage. Mike was helping him, handing him what he asked for. Jo was gazing at the spectacle too, so only Sam noticed when wisps of yellow-tinged gas suddenly started to boil out of the second fumarole. It bubbled up from inside the hole and then churned around faster as it leaked up into the sky.

'Dad,' he began, 'what –'

A roaring sound drowned out his words. Gas shot into the sky in a column that enveloped the helicopter and it lurched violently, throwing Sam forward against his seat belt. Mike yelled something.

Yellowish clouds billowed upwards, cutting off the view. There was a sudden reek of gas. Sam felt his eyes stinging and starting to water. He tried to hold his breath, but he had to gasp for air and he choked as the stuff got into his mouth and lungs. Jo was crouched in the seat beside him, her hands over her face, coughing.

The helicopter swung away from the slope, clearing the worst of the clouds. Zack was fighting the controls. The engine spluttered and died. Sam caught a dizzying glimpse of grey rock sliding past, and then the tops of trees rushing up to meet them.

'We're going to crash!'

CHAPTER TWO

Just as Sam thought the helicopter would plunge into the trees, the engine fired unevenly and the downward motion stopped. They skimmed over the forest at a crazy angle, heading back towards the cone. Zack yelled, 'The air-feed's blocked!'

'Hold on, everybody!' yelled Russ.

Sam braced himself for the crash. Grey rock filled his vision, but at the last second Zack managed to veer away. They spun back across the forest. The sound of the rotor blades, so smooth that previously Sam had stopped noticing it, had grown irregular as the engine kept on missing and picking up again.

The air in the cabin began to clear; Sam wiped his streaming eyes and saw Jo beside him, white-faced, clinging to her seat and staring out at the trees rushing by below. Mike was huddled in his seat, hiding his face.

'Dad,' Sam said, 'what should we do?'

'Nothing,' Russ said. 'Keep hanging on. It'll be OK.'

Sam didn't believe him. But there was nothing else to do.

Zack glanced over his shoulder and raised his voice above the stuttering of the blades. 'I'll have to put her down. Be ready and do as I tell you, right?'

'Right,' said Russ.

As his father spoke, Sam saw a gap open up in the trees below, a narrow valley with a stream at the bottom. It was carpeted with undergrowth and the slope was steep, but it looked as if it might be safe to land.

His momentary hope died as Zack said, 'Listen – we're going to hit. Best if you folks get out first.'

Jo started to protest, but the helicopter pitched again and she slapped a hand across her mouth as if she wanted to stop herself from screaming.

'I'll bring her down real low, right?' Zack said. 'And then, when I say jump, jump.'

In a series of jerks and lurches the helicopter descended until it was wallowing over the tops of the bushes. Russ crawled out of his seat and tugged the hatch open. 'Mike, you first.'

Mike stumbled over to the opening and crouched on the edge, staring at the ground as it slid by below.

'Jump!' Zack yelled.

'I can't,' Mike said.

'Yes, you can.' Jo flung herself at him. 'Go, Mike! Fall like you do in judo class.'

Not waiting for him to agree, she gave him a shove. His shout was cut off; Sam saw him crash into the undergrowth. By then, Jo had flipped out neatly after him.

Russ grinned at Sam. 'Feisty girl, that. Come on, your turn.'

Sam didn't like the idea at all, but he wasn't going to mess about, not when Jo had been so unexpectedly slick. He gave a quick glance downwards, curled himself up with his head tucked under folded arms, and rolled out of the hatch.

There was a second's free fall, and then stems were snapping around him, raking over his arms and legs and catching in his clothes. The breath was driven out of him as he hit the ground. He felt himself sliding and he uncurled himself, snatching wildly for something he could hold on to. His fingers closed round something that felt like rope, and his arm was wrenched as he came to a stop.

A thunderclap reverberated all around him, as if the world was splitting apart. The helicopter, Sam thought dazedly, half expecting the wreckage to crash down on top of him. He lay, frozen, until the noise died away and everything was still. Only then did he realize that since his jump he had kept his eyes tight shut.

He opened them now. He was lying splayed out across the slope, one hand gripping the stem of a vine. Huge leaves arched over him; the light was dim and green. Painfully, he sat up and poked his head out.

The first thing he saw was the helicopter, half buried in the opposite slope. Its rotor blades had buckled. The windows were smashed and glittering scraps of perspex had sprayed down into the stream. The cabin was folded inwards and the tail rotor had sheared off.

Sam knelt there, staring blankly, until his mind started working again. Then he shouted hoarsely, 'Dad! Dad!'

He gazed wildly from side to side. Further up the slope, Jo was on her feet, giving Mike a hand to stand up. Both of them looked battered, but at least they were able to move.

Sam still couldn't see his father. 'Dad!' he called again.

He thought he heard an answering shout. A patch of foliage closer to the stream began thrashing about, and Russ appeared out of it, scrambling to his feet with his arms wrapped round the bag of camera gear.

'Dad, are you OK?' Sam called. He skidded down the slope towards his father. Blood was trickling from a scrape down the side of Russ's face. He grabbed Sam's arm as he came up to him. 'Are you hurt?'

'No, Dad, I'm fine,' Sam said automatically, but he wasn't too sure about that. His body felt like one big bruise, his arms and legs were scratched and his T-shirt was torn – but at least he could walk and his head was clear.

He watched Jo and Mike carefully picking their way down the slope to join them. There was no sign of anyone else on either side of the stream. Sam shaded his eyes from the sun and peered up at the helicopter.

'Dad – do you think Zack's still in there?'

Russ had crouched beside the stream and was sluicing blood and grit from his face and hands. He didn't reply. Sam's eyes went back to the opposite slope. That side was steeper, rising to a ridge just above the place where the helicopter had crashed. It would be a tough climb, especially when they were all still shocked from the jump.

Putting it out of his mind for the moment, Sam turned to Jo and Mike as they approached. Jo was limping, and Mike cradled one arm with the other hand. 'What's the matter?' Sam asked.

Jo pulled a face as she stood on one foot and flexed the other foot and ankle. 'Nothing. I jarred it, falling. It'll be OK, I think. Mike's cut his arm, though. Wash it in the stream, Mike,' she said, turning to her brother.

Mike knelt down and did as Jo told him. There seemed to be a lot of blood, though Sam was relieved that the arm wasn't broken. 'Dad, what do you think we should do?' he asked.

Russ Carlsen got up, dabbing at his face with a handkerchief. 'Get up there,' he said, gesturing towards the helicopter. 'See if we can find Zack. There should be a first-aid kit, and maybe we can get off a distress call on the radio.'

His mention of the distress call made Sam think for the first time beyond the immediate emergency. They were all alive, and more or less unhurt. Except possibly for Zack, he thought, with a sudden sick feeling in his stomach. But that wasn't the end of their problems. Somehow they had to get off the island.

'Isn't there a village?' Jo asked. 'Somewhere we could phone? And maybe get a wash?' She looked down disgustedly at her shorts and T-shirt, torn and stained with grass and soil.

'Sorry.' Russ spread his arms apologetically. 'Totally uninhabited. What you see is what you get.'

Jo sniffed. Sam hid a grin. He would never have admitted it, but he was quite impressed by how Jo was taking this. He'd have expected her to panic more – not just fuss about her ruined clothes.

'OK,' said Sam. 'Let's get going. How're you doing, Mike?'

Mike looked up from the side of the stream. He had washed the cut clean, but blood was still oozing out of it. He looked ashen white and miserable. 'All right,' he said, but he didn't sound as if he meant it.

'I bet it hurts,' Sam said sympathetically.

Jo fished in her pocket for a handkerchief and bound it tightly round the cut. 'It'll do till we get a proper bandage,' she said.

Mike stood up, holding the arm stiffly. 'Mr Carlsen,' he said, 'they will come and get us, won't they?'

'Of course they will,' Russ said. 'Liz knows where we are, and your mum and dad. Even if we can't get a distress call off, they'll come looking for us sooner or later.'

'We'll make camp by the helicopter,' Sam added, trying to cheer Mike up. 'They're bound to see us there.'

He led the way upstream until he found a place where he could cross by balancing on stones jutting out of the water. Jo followed, helping Mike, and Russ brought up the rear, poking about in his camera bag to see how his equipment had survived the fall.

While Sam waited for them, he thought he could hear a rumbling sound, coming from somewhere up above, and feel a faint shuddering under his feet. He looked up to where he could just see the grey crags rising to the volcano's cone. Plumes of smoke were rising high into the air, but there was no sign of anything that could have made the noise.

Jo was looking up as well. 'Did you hear that?'

'What was it?' Mike asked.

Sam shrugged. 'Dunno. Thunder, maybe.'

He knew as he spoke how stupid that was. There wasn't a cloud in the sky.

Jo jumped from the last stone to the bank at his side and said, 'I thought at first it might be somebody looking for us. Another helicopter. But it didn't sound like an engine.'

'Maybe volcanoes make funny noises.'

Russ joined them on the far bank of the stream. He said nothing about the noise, and Sam didn't want to go on talking about it in case Mike got even more scared.

'Listen,' Russ said. 'I've been thinking. The helicopter must be leaking fuel. It could catch fire or even blow up. Let me go up there first and check it out. You wait here.'

Without waiting for a reply, he set off up the slope, using his hands to pull himself up the steeper parts. Sam watched him go. Jo and Mike squatted on the bank.

The rumbling sound came again. This time it grew louder, swelling to a roar. Halfway up the slope, Russ straightened. Then he spun round. 'Sam!' he yelled. 'Everybody! Get up here! Fast!'

Skidding, half falling, he scrambled back towards them. Sam stared upwards. Along the gully, where the stream had flowed peacefully among the stones, a huge wall of mud exploded into sight. Branches were being tossed around in it; foam frothed brown against the sky. The air was suddenly heavy with the reek of sulphur.

Sam stood, frozen, as the flood bore down towards him.

CHAPTER THREE

'**S**am! Snap out of it!' Russ yelled. He grabbed Sam's arm and thrust him towards the slope. 'Up! Jo, Mike, get up here! Fast!'

Sam saw Jo push Mike upwards and his father gave the younger boy a hand. He came out of his momentary shock. Grabbing frantically at stones and plant stems, he forced himself to climb, faster and faster as the mud swept with a thundering roar down the gully, filling it.

He saw mud rush past his feet and knew he had not escaped yet. The level was rising all the time. He needed to get higher – away from the churning brown ooze. Breath sobbing, arms and legs aching, he hauled himself away from the engulfing mud.

Behind him, a scream cut through the roar of the flood. Sam glanced round. His dad and Mike were level with him; just below, Jo had lost her footing on the edge of the mud. As it surged over her, Sam saw her grab at a clump of overhanging leaves, but they gave way under her weight. She screamed again as the mud swept her away.

Mike shouted, 'Jo! Jo!' and started to climb down towards her.

Russ snapped at him, 'No, stay here. Sam, keep him out of this.' He shoved his camera bag into Sam's arms and flung himself down the slope, sliding on a diagonal, trying to intercept Jo further down.

Sam dumped the bag. Whatever his dad said, he couldn't just stand and watch. 'Come on,' he said to Mike.

He started to scramble crab-wise across the slope, trying to stay above the mud but stay abreast of his dad and Jo further down. The level had stopped rising, he thought, or at least it was rising very slowly now, and the terrifying thunder was dying away into a low, rushing noise.

Jo was still in sight, her face a white blob against the mud, one arm free and waving wildly, but the torrent was sweeping her down too fast for Russ to catch her.

'She'll sink!' Mike screamed.

Panting, Sam said, 'Keep going.'

'It's no good! We can't do anything.'

A curve in the gully took Jo out of sight. A moment later, Russ disappeared over the shoulder of the hill.

'Cut across!' Sam yelled to Mike. 'We might catch her further down.'

He laboured up to the top of the rise and stood there, panting. Just below, the slope grew steeper still and then it levelled out until it disappeared under the surface of the mud flow. Russ was squatting down on the edge.

'Where's Jo?' Mike gasped.

Sam thought he heard a faint cry, but he wasn't sure where it came from. He slid down towards his father. The mud flow was running more slowly now, the surface churning like soup. As Sam drew closer, he saw Jo, a few metres upstream of Russ, being carried down to where he was waiting. Only her head and one arm were visible; her face and hair were plastered with mud, as if her head had gone under, but she was still alive.

Sam let out a cry of relief. 'Mike, she's here!'

Russ was reaching out to her. Jo strained to catch hold of his hand, but Sam could see that she was going to be swept past.

'Help! I can't reach!' she cried.

As she came level with him, Russ floundered a few paces into the mud and caught hold of her outstretched arm. For a few seconds they clung together; the mud came up to Russ's chest, and Sam could see that he was going to be carried off his feet.

'Dad!' he yelled.

Sam skidded to a stop at the edge of the mud flow. Mike was panting just behind him. Sam gazed wildly around and caught sight of a scrawny bush growing a metre or so away from the edge. 'Mike! Grab hold of that!'

Mike saw what he meant. He grasped one of the branches and held his other hand out to Sam. They gripped each other's wrists, and Sam stepped cautiously out into the mud.

He could feel the suction as he edged out to where his father was still fighting to keep his balance and hang on to Jo at the same time. Russ grinned and held out a hand. 'Great, Sam,' he said. 'Just take it slowly.'

Sam waded out another couple of steps. The mud was up to his knees. His arms and Mike's were at full stretch now. 'Mike, don't let go!' he warned.

Then he felt his dad's fingers fasten round his wrist. There was a sudden wrench as Sam took the extra weight.

'OK,' Russ said. 'Pull us in. Steady.'

At first Sam thought he couldn't move. The mud was pushing against him, wanting to tear him away from his grip on Mike. He forced himself to take a step back towards the bank. Then another. He could hear his breath coming in rapid gasps. Another step back. He was almost clear of the stuff by now, and the level had sunk to his dad's waist.

Russ had an arm round Jo, keeping her head and shoulders clear of the mud. She managed a weak grin, and said, 'Go, Sam.'

Mike cried out, 'Sam, the branch!'

Not looking, Sam made one massive

effort and threw himself backwards. He felt his dad release him. With a horrible sucking sound the mud let him go; he stumbled on to solid ground and lost his grip on Mike as he fell to his knees. Jo had found her feet; she and Russ floundered back to the edge together and collapsed, side by side, on the bank. Sam glanced back at Mike; the younger boy was standing beside the bush, staring at the branch that had come away in his hands.

Russ was sitting with his head in his hands. Jo lay, face down, her body heaving as she took in deep gulps of air.

'Jo!' Mike said, kneeling beside her. 'Jo, are you all right?'

After a minute, his sister rolled over and reached out to give his arm a shake. 'No, I'm not. I'm filthy and exhausted and I've swallowed about a gallon of that stuff.'

Mike suddenly grinned widely. 'She's OK!'

Jo sat up and rubbed her hands over her face and hair, shaking off great clots of mud. 'I said I wanted a wash, not a mud bath.' Serious suddenly, she added, 'Thanks. All of you.'

Sam just felt relieved that she was safe.

There was more to Jo than he'd thought at first. She really had guts; if nothing else, the crisis had shown him that.

'What I don't understand,' he said, 'is where all that mud came from. It hasn't rained for ages.'

'Well . . . there's only one place where we've seen that much water,' said Russ.

'The crater lake?'

His dad nodded. 'If the crater wall collapsed, the water would rush out and pick up soil and rock on its way. It's a well-known volcanic phenomenon,' he added. 'They call it a lahar.'

'Mr Carlsen,' Jo said in a dead-pan voice, 'you've no idea how much better I feel, knowing that.'

'Then what made the crater wall collapse?' Mike asked. 'Is the volcano going to erupt?'

Sam spun round and stared up at the cone, but it remained grey and silent, still wreathed in smoke. He had always thought that volcanic eruptions meant ash and molten lava, not mud. Tangaroa showed no signs of producing those. At least, not yet, he thought to himself.

'I don't know,' said Russ, in reply to Mike's question. 'But if there is going to be trouble, then the best we can do is get back to the helicopter and send off a distress call.'

When Jo felt fit to move, they started back. She waved Russ away when he offered to help her. 'Honestly. I'm fine now.'

The mud flow was slowing, and it had not risen any higher. Whatever had set it off was over, for the time being at least. If Tangaroa had any more nasty surprises for them, Sam didn't want to think about them.

'I should get some pictures of this,' Russ said. 'Sam, give me the – Sam, what have you done with my camera bag?'

'I left it back there.' Sam gestured towards the slope below the helicopter. 'I had to hurry to help Jo.'

Russ grunted. 'Sam, if you've lost my gear, I'll ground you for the rest of your life.' He hurried on ahead.

Jo laughed. 'I like your dad,' she said. 'He's cool.'

'He's crazy. As if I really care about being grounded right now!'

While Russ retrieved the bag, Sam and

the others made straight for the crashed
helicopter.

'I guess if it hasn't blown up already it's
not going to,' said Sam.

As he climbed the last few metres up to
the wreck, he began wondering uneasily
what he was going to find. If Zack was still
inside, he must be unconscious at best. Sam
didn't know what to do for someone who
was seriously hurt. He was trying not to let
himself think about the possibility that Zack
was dead.

When they reached the helicopter, Jo
flopped down on the ground to rest, and
Mike sat beside her. Russ was climbing back
up the slope, hampered by the heavy camera
bag. Sam didn't want to wait. Swallowing
hard, he pulled himself up to the hatch,
which was jammed open. Inside, the
passenger seats were squashed tight together;
Sam shuddered at the realization that if they
had stayed there, they would have been
crushed.

Sam crawled inside, trying to force his
way forward to the pilot's seat. The
helicopter shifted a little under his weight,
but it was firmly wedged among the rocks.

Before Sam got half way, he could see what he needed to know. The pilot's seat was empty. There was no sign of Zack.

'Sam!' It was his father's voice, still at a distance. 'Sam, I said I'd go in there.'

'I'm fine!' Sam called back, starting to wriggle his way out again.

'Can you see Zack?'

'No.' Sam scrambled out backwards and dropped to the ground as Russ came up. 'He's not there. I don't know where he is.'

Russ glanced over his shoulder at the mud flow that was still pouring sluggishly down the valley. 'If he jumped out when we did . . .'

Sam felt cold. 'He might have been unconscious. We wouldn't have seen him if he was under the bushes.'

'You mean he's under there now?' said Jo.

'I don't know,' said Sam. 'He might be.'

His dad started to shout Zack's name again, but there was no reply, apart from the rushing of the mud flow. Jo turned her face away. At last Russ stopped shouting; his shoulders sagged.

'Listen, Dad,' Sam said, 'We've got to think ahead. What about the distress call?

And we said we'd look for a first-aid kit for Mike's arm.'

'My arm's OK,' said Mike determinedly.

'We still ought to fix it,' Jo said.

'I'll go in again,' said Sam.

'No, I'll do it,' Mike offered, rather to Sam's surprise. 'I'm the smallest, I can wriggle through the seats. And if I can get to the radio I know how to send off a distress call.'

'Are you sure?' Russ asked.

'Oh, yes,' said Jo. 'He's a real electronics whizz, aren't you, Mike?'

Mike went red and swatted at her, embarrassed.

'Go on, then,' said Russ. 'But be careful. And if I tell you to get out, you get out. No arguments, OK?'

'OK.'

Mike gripped the edge of the hatch, hauled himself up, and slid forward along the floor of the cabin. For a minute his legs waved in the air; then he got a toehold on the edge of the hatch and pushed himself further in. He vanished; Sam could still hear the rattle of loose metal as he moved on.

'I hope he doesn't get stuck,' he said.

A few minutes later, there was a scraping sound, and Mike's voice saying, 'Here.'

Sam saw his foot pushing a metal box back towards the hatch. His dad reached up and captured it. 'First-aid kit,' he said. 'Well done, Mike.'

Russ searched through the first-aid kit to find a dressing for Mike's arm. Sam squatted on the ground while he waited, looking out across the mud river and the trees on the other side of the valley. Everything was quiet now. He couldn't help wondering if it was too quiet, as if the whole island was brooding, waiting for something.

He looked up. 'Dad?' Then he shook himself. He was being stupid, imagining things. If he started talking about the volcano, about whether it might erupt, he would only scare Jo and Mike. And if it did erupt, talking wouldn't do any good. The only thing that would help was the distress call that Mike was working on now.

'What's up, Sam?' his dad asked.

'Nothing.'

'Because I reckon that –' He broke off and swung round as Mike's voice came from the helicopter.

'Mr Carlsen? I'm sorry, I've tried sending the signal, but the radio won't work. We can't tell anyone we're here.'

CHAPTER FOUR

Just for a moment, Mike sounded panicky again.

'Steady on,' said Russ. 'Do you want me to come and have a look?'

'I don't think you could get in here,' Mike said. 'Just a minute . . .'

Jo got to her feet and tried to look in through the hatch. 'Mike, are you OK in there?'

No reply, except for a few rattling and scraping noises. Then Mike's voice came again, sounding relieved. 'I'm fine, Jo. I was just looking to see if there's a toolkit, and there is. I reckon I can fix the radio, but I'm going to try to get it out first. It'll be easier to work on if I haven't got my knees in my mouth.'

Jo laughed. 'Let Mike near a screwdriver, and he's happy for hours.'

'Great,' said Russ. 'Mike, let us know if there's anything we can do to help.'

While they waited, Russ motioned to Sam and Jo to sit beside him on the slope. 'I'd just as soon talk where Mike can't hear us,' he began. 'I don't want to scare him. But we have to make some decisions.'

'Like what to do about Zack?' Sam asked.

'Yes. It's just possible he got out and went over the ridge.'

'Then why didn't he hear us shouting?' Sam liked to think that Zack was still alive, but he was beginning to feel that there wasn't much hope.

'Maybe he's unconscious. We'll take a look in a minute, but first . . .'

'You think Tangaroa's going to erupt, don't you?' Jo asked.

Russ shook his head, frowning. 'I don't know. It sounds stupid . . . there's not been an eruption this century.'

Sam jerked his head in the direction of the

mud flow. 'There hasn't been one of those, either, has there? Look, Dad, if Tangaroa blows, I don't want to be around. If we can't get off the island, at least we can get further away from the cone.'

Sam was surprised to hear himself sound so determined. All he knew was that he was getting more scared by the minute of the stark grey slopes up above. He was even more surprised to see his dad and Jo nodding in agreement.

'We'll have a last look for Zack,' said Russ. 'We'll wait to see if Mike can do anything with the radio –'

'And then we're outta here,' Jo finished for him.

While she was speaking, there was more rattling from inside the helicopter, and Mike appeared, crawling out, feet first.

Sam got to his feet and went over to the hatch.

'Here,' Mike said, pushing a canvas backpack past himself and into Sam's hands. 'I thought this might come in handy.'

Sam grabbed the backpack and looked inside. It was obviously Zack's personal property. Inside were a couple of cans of soft drink and a slab of chocolate. 'Hey, great!' he said, showing his dad and Jo.

'I don't suppose Zack would mind,' said Jo. 'I'd kill for a drink.'

'We'd better be careful, though,' said Russ. 'We don't know how long this might have to last us.'

He opened one can; they handed it round, taking a mouthful each. Sam hadn't thought much about being thirsty until then, but he could taste mud and sulphurous gases in his mouth, and the sharp orange bite of the drink was delicious.

It reminded him that he was starting to feel hungry. If everything had gone well, they would have been heading back for lunch by now. Instead, Sam had no idea when he would get his next proper meal; he tried not to think about it.

Meanwhile, Mike came scrabbling backwards through the hatch, the radio held carefully between his hands. He laid it on the ground, pulled out a small toolkit from his back pocket, and set to work. When Jo handed him the can, he took a swig absentmindedly and gave it back without taking his eyes off the radio. Sam was impressed by the expert way he began taking off the cover to expose the components inside.

'If it can be fixed, he'll fix it,' said Jo. 'But if something vital's broken . . .' She shrugged and finished off the drink, putting the can tidily back inside the helicopter. 'Leave nothing but footprints,' she said primly. 'Take nothing but memories.'

'And photographs,' said Russ, grinning. He took out his camera, checked the settings, and began to take some shots of the mud flow. There was nothing anyone could do to help Mike except leave him to get on in peace.

'Jo,' said Russ, when he had taken several pictures, 'why don't you have a rest? Sam and I will climb up to the top of the ridge and see if we can see anything of Zack.'

'Sure.' Jo lay down beside her brother, folded her hands behind her head, and closed her eyes.

Sam followed Russ up the final stretch of the slope until they stood on the ridge.

Behind them, to the north of the island, was the cone of the volcano. From here, the grey shape looked smudged; Sam realized that smoke and gas were pouring out of the fumaroles, and from the crater in the centre. The clouds coiled sluggishly in the still air.

'Dad . . .' he said uneasily. Russ glanced upwards, grunted, and then raised his camera to take a picture. 'Dad, that's really not helping.'

'Well, it helps me,' retorted Russ. 'It's what I do. Besides,' he added, lowering the camera, 'when we get out of here, these pictures will be very useful. Not just for me to sell, I don't mean that. For scientists trying to study volcanoes. If they don't help us, they might help somebody else some time.'

'Yeah, sure,' said Sam. 'Now let's look for Zack, huh?'

He turned away from the cone and stared out in the other direction. On one side was the narrow valley where the helicopter had come down, partly filled now with the lahar that was still oozing down the channel of the stream. On the other side, a gentler slope led downwards into another valley, much wider and shallower than the first. A luxuriant growth of trees and shrubs covered the ground – palm trees and banana plants with their wide, flat leaves, and others that Sam could not put a name to. In the distance he could just make out the blue line of the sea. It looked very peaceful and came almost as a shock after the danger they had already been through.

Sam took a few steps down the slope on the far side.

'Watch your feet,' Russ warned him. 'There might be snakes.'

'That's all we need,' Sam muttered.

His feet were sinking into the rich vegetation, and he couldn't be sure that it was safe to walk there. He realized how difficult it would be to find Zack if he was lying unconscious somewhere in this undergrowth. They might search for a week and still not know whether they had missed him. He tried looking for some disturbance that might show where Zack had trampled down the plants or had fallen among them, but there was nothing obvious. He shouted Zack's name several times, but there was no reply.

Over to Sam's left, Russ was working his way across the slope, using a branch to poke under bushes and through the overhanging curtains of vines. Sam wondered whether he risked disturbing something nasty; a few birds flew up, cackling a protest, but there was nothing else. And no sign of Zack.

Sam set off in the opposite direction, covering the slope in a wide sweep, until at last he met his father in the middle. 'This is hopeless,' he said.

Russ pushed his hair back; sweat was plastering it to his forehead. 'You're right. If he's conscious, he would have heard us. If he's unconscious, we'll never find him. If he's here at all.'

'You think the mud caught him, don't you?' Sam asked.

Russ hesitated, his mouth tightening. 'Yes, Sam. I do.' He threw the branch away. 'Come on, let's see how Mike's doing.'

As he turned away, Sam took a last look across the slope. He knew his dad was right, but it was hard to give up the search when they could be leaving Zack to die of his injuries.

When Sam and his dad reached the top of the ridge again, Mike and Jo were still sitting beside the helicopter. Jo had the first-aid kit open and was fixing a dressing over the cut on Mike's arm.

Mike waved with his free hand. 'I think I got through!' he called.

'You *think*?' Sam said, making his way down the slope to join them.

'Yeah.' Mike made a face. 'I found the frequency for the rescue service, and I started talking to somebody, but there was a lot of static, and then I lost them again. I don't know how much they heard.'

'Well, it's a start,' said Russ.

'I'll have another go in a minute,' said Mike, glancing at Jo, who was tying a bandage on his arm.

'All done,' she said, adding to Sam, 'You didn't find Zack?'

Sam shook his head. Jo looked down at the mud; Sam could guess what she was thinking. She had nearly been swallowed by it; Zack would have had no chance at all if he had been lying unconscious in the bottom of the valley.

'Look,' Russ said briskly, 'we've done all we can to look for him. I don't think there's any point in hanging around here any longer. Sam's right; we'll be safer if we get away from the cone.'

'I think we should go that way,' Sam said,

gesturing towards the ridge. 'It looked as if the slope leads straight down to the sea. If we're on the beach, a rescue boat would be able to see us, or a helicopter.'

'What about the radio?' Mike asked.

'We'll take it with us,' said Russ. 'Whenever we take a rest, you can try to get through again.'

While they were talking, Jo had packed up the first-aid equipment, and she went to fetch Zack's backpack. Mike fitted the radio and the toolkit inside and settled the pack on his shoulders. Sam guessed that Mike thought the radio was his responsibility and therefore he insisted on carrying it.

'OK, let's go,' said Russ.

They climbed the slope to the ridge. Sam turned at the top to look back for the last time at the helicopter. Somehow it felt wrong to be leaving it. What might have happened to Zack was still weighing on his mind. If he was dead, then no one could help him; but they still couldn't be sure he wasn't lying hurt somewhere. Sam didn't like the thought of leaving anyone if there was still a chance of his surviving.

The others had begun to descend the far

slope, down into the valley and towards the sea.

'Sam!' Russ called. 'Are you daydreaming?'

Sam turned and started to follow, but before he could catch up with the others he heard a loud rattling sound, just as if somebody was shaking enormous dice. 'Dad!' he yelled.

Everyone stopped, staring at the grey slopes above.

The rattling grew to a continuous roar. Sam hunched his shoulders against it as if it was a physical blow.

From the cone of the volcano a pillar of fire and ash blasted upwards. Black and dull red, it rose high into the air and began to spread across the sky. There was no mistaking what was happening.

Tangaroa was erupting.

CHAPTER FIVE

The column of ash and flame roared and billowed into the sky. Smoke boiled into a mushroom cloud that shut out the sunlight. Lightning flickered across it.

For a few seconds, everyone stood still, faces turned upwards, watching. A wave of heat rolled over them as the ground shuddered beneath their feet. The noise of the blast filled the sky.

Sam felt oddly calm, as if it didn't have anything to do with him. Something quiet inside him was saying, 'Well, this is it.'

Russ stared with his mouth open. Then, almost as if he wasn't thinking about it, he raised his camera and took a couple of quick shots.

Jo was the first to move. She grabbed Mike and spun him round, back in the direction they were taking. 'Go, Mike!' she shouted.

'No!' Just before following them, Sam had taken a last, quick glance up the valley. What he saw brought him to a halt, waving wildly to the others to get back up on to the ridge. Something else was flowing down from the direction of the cone.

It came fast; almost as soon as Sam called, it reached the slopes just below the cone. At first he thought it was more mud, but although it looked like liquid it was grey at the edges, reddish-purple at the core, and it swept down the valley in an eerie silence.

The reek of sulphur filled the air again. Sam began to cough as it caught him in the back of the throat; his eyes stung and there was a metallic taste in his mouth.

'What is it?' Mike gasped, as Sam grabbed him and hauled him back on to the ridge.

'Ash,' said Russ. 'Ash and . . . gas.'

He and Jo crowded up beside the two boys, and they huddled together on the highest point between the two valleys, watching the grey flow rush past them. Sam could see huge boulders inside it, bounding along like tennis balls, rolled along by the surge of gas. The cloud was curling and boiling upwards, so that he was afraid they weren't high enough to escape it. But there was nowhere else to go.

The undergrowth flamed as it passed, and the silence gave way to the crackling of fire. Some trees began to go up like torches, others were knocked out of the ground and carried along with the flood. Within seconds the whole valley was ablaze.

Sam had his arms round Jo and Mike. He could feel them both shaking. He wanted to run and hide, or at least crouch on the ground and hide his head. But he knew how useless that would be. Somehow they had to get away. But the route they had meant to take was now a blazing pit of volcanic ash.

'Dad!' he called, trying to make himself heard over the continuing roar from the cone.

Russ had his camera to his eye again, but he turned at Sam's voice. He wore a fiercely determined look, as if nothing was going to stop him recording all this on film.

'Dad!' Sam yelled again. Suddenly he was furious. He had the urge to grab his dad's camera and throw it down into the ash. 'Dad, what are we going to do?'

Russ opened his mouth to reply, but his words were lost in a sudden ripping sound. A fireball shot out from the cone. Huge and flaring red, it soared overhead and buried itself in the mud, sending up a hissing cloud of steam. Instinctively Sam ducked, lost his balance and fell, pulling Jo and Mike down with him. A fusillade of smaller fire-bombs fell just short of them, spattering over the ground and on the roof of the helicopter. The vegetation around them caught fire and the flames began creeping towards them from the valley below.

Jo started scrabbling her way down towards the helicopter. 'Come on!' she shouted. 'We can shelter in there!'

Instinctively Sam grabbed her and held her back. 'No!' he yelled.

'But the fireballs will hit us!'

'Just listen, will you?'

Somehow Sam could see what was going

to happen. If they went back to the helicopter – even supposing they could all squeeze into the wrecked cabin – they would be trapped. All the stories he had heard about being buried under volcanic ash like the people at Pompeii whirled through his mind. Two thousand years ago they were smothered where they stood, their faces twisted into horrible death-masks.

'It's not safe!' he gasped. 'If we hide in there, the fire will cut us off. The ash will cover us. We've got to get away!'

Mike was still crouching on the ground with his arms wrapped round his head. Sam hauled him to his feet and pushed him along the spine of the ridge. Flanked on one side by the mud flow and on the other by fire and ash, it was the only way out. Sam didn't know where it would lead, but they didn't have a choice. He clutched at Jo's arm and shoved her along, still protesting, after her brother.

'Dad!' he shouted.

Russ Carlsen still had his camera raised, snapping off shot after shot, while more volcanic debris rained down all around. 'Amazing!' he said. 'We'll never see anything like this again.'

'We'll never see *anything* again if you don't get a move on.'

Russ started and seemed to come out of his trance. He let go the camera, to dangle by its strap. 'Right – lead on.'

'Follow Jo and Mike!' Sam pointed along the ridge where the others could just be seen in the thickening air. Russ headed after them, and Sam stumbled along in the rear. For a few seconds he struggled with hysterical laughter. He felt like a sheepdog trying to round up a bunch of awkward sheep.

Tangaroa still threw out its fire.

Glancing over his shoulder, Sam could see the pillar of dull flame at the centre of the eruption; around it, all was dark. The ash and gases from the centre of the volcano had blackened all the sky and cut off his view of the upper parts of the mountain. Waves of heat rolled off the burning trees. Sam fled behind his dad, with flaming debris spitting all around him.

As he struggled to put as much distance between himself and the cone as he could, he heard a soft, explosive sound behind him. He whirled round, to see the helicopter burst into flames and then detach itself from the slope where it had crashed and turn slowly over and over before it hit the mud and began to sink.

CHAPTER SIX

Sam and his dad caught up with Jo and Mike and the four of them blundered along the ridge in growing darkness, their way lit only by the fire in the valley alongside.

The ash from the eruption was beginning to fall to earth, filling the air around them. Sam felt as if he couldn't breathe; his chest heaved as he tried to gulp in air, but at the same time he was terrified that the glowing sparks would sear his throat and his lungs. It hurt to cough, but he couldn't stop himself.

They had not gone far when Mike halted, doubled over and choking helplessly. Jo put an arm round him, but there was nothing she could do for him.

'Here.' Russ handed her a cleaning cloth from his camera bag. 'Tie that round his nose and mouth. It might help.'

Jo did as he suggested. 'Come on, Mike, you'll be fine,' she said comfortingly. 'You look like a real gangster.'

After a minute, Mike straightened up. He was panting and his breath rasped, but the choking fit had passed. 'Thanks,' he managed to say. 'I'm OK now.'

He was still carrying Zack's backpack; Sam felt annoyed with himself for not thinking that the weight would be too much for him. Now he lifted it off and fitted it on his own back. 'My turn,' he said, forcing a grin.

Meanwhile, Russ had tied his handkerchief over his own face; Sam pulled up his T-shirt to cover his nose and mouth and, when she was sure Mike was fit to carry on, Jo did the same. Sam wished he could cover his eyes as well; he screwed them up against the hot ash and hoped that would be enough.

They struggled on. Already the ash was

starting to cover the ground like a fall of black snow. It was hot to walk on, even through the soles of their shoes, and as it grew thicker each step became more uncomfortable.

The ridge was flattening out. The heat abated slightly as the burning valley was left behind. Sam thought, too, that they were beginning to descend, though the slope was so gradual he could not be sure. He cheered up a little to think that they were getting closer to the beach, but he was no longer sure if that would do any good. It might be too dangerous for a rescue boat or a helicopter to venture close to the island, and even if anyone was looking for them they might not be able to see them through the thick clouds of volcanic debris. Sam tried to think of some way they could make a signal to show where they were, but the only thought that filled his mind was a determination to keep going.

The ash was becoming more painful underfoot, as if the soles of their shoes were burning away. Sam needed to rest – he knew they all did – but for some time he couldn't see a place where they could stop safely. Then as he peered from side to side he noticed an outcrop of rock poking up from the ash-covered ground, some way to the left. He grabbed Jo's arm and pointed. 'Let's get up there – rest for a bit.'

'OK.'

She veered off in the direction of the outcrop, and the others followed. The rocks were black, volcanic, slanting out of the ground. As Sam had hoped, the angle was so steep that not much of the ash had settled on it. They were able to scramble up for a brief respite.

Jo pulled the trainer from one of her feet and tipped a stream of ash out of it. 'Look at that,' she said disgustedly. 'Those were new for this holiday.'

Sam nearly said something rude, about thinking of her shoes at a time like this, until he realized she was trying to keep everybody's spirits up. Not very well, maybe, but at least she was trying. 'Designer gear, huh?' he said, with an attempt at a grin.

'Yeah – specially for climbing down volcanoes.' She dabbed experimentally at the sole. 'It's starting to melt!'

Sam examined his own trainers and tipped out the ash. Jo was right. What if they melt right through? he wondered silently. 'New fashion – sticky feet,' he said.

Mike laughed, but the laughter turned into a coughing fit. Ash was still falling gently around them, sifting over them where they huddled on the rocks. Sam could see they wouldn't be able to rest for long.

It was so dark they could only see a little way ahead.

'I wish we knew which way to go,' said Sam.

'Away from that,' his dad replied, jerking his head in the direction of the blast. 'And down. That's the best we can do.'

Sam knew he was right, but as they set off again he couldn't help worrying.

They slogged on through ash that grew thicker by the minute. Soon the downward slope grew steeper and became broken up into rough steps, with more rock showing through. Sam wondered if they were climbing down an old lava flow. As the rock grew higher on either side of them, he became convinced that nothing else could have twisted it into such strange shapes.

The going became slightly easier as the rock walls gave them some shelter. After a while they came to a place where the rock was hollowed out with an overhang like the roof of a cave. Jo staggered under it and curled herself up, with her arms round her knees and her back to the wall.

'Let's take another break,' she said.

It was a good place. Beneath the rock, the coating of ash was thin and, although the shrubs that grew on top of the overhang were blackened with ash, they had not caught fire. Sam and Mike crowded in beside Jo; in spite of the darkness Russ paused to take another photograph.

'Dad,' said Sam, 'if that camera is the slightest bit of use to us, I'll eat it.'

His dad gave him a tired grin. 'I wouldn't let you. It's a good one.'

When he was settled in the cave, Sam slipped off the backpack so that he could rest more comfortably, and he remembered the second can of drink, still untouched. 'Does anyone want a drink?' he asked.

Just the question made him realize how fiercely thirsty he was. Mike looked longingly at the backpack, but Jo said, 'We might need it more, later on. We can manage for a bit longer.'

Sam had to agree with her and he tried to put the sharp orange taste out of his mind. He remembered the iced drink he had sucked through straws beside the pool that morning, and how bored he had felt. He wouldn't have objected to feeling bored now.

He peered at his watch and realized that it was barely four hours since the helicopter had taken off from the airfield. Sam wouldn't have believed that things could change so quickly, and that in such a short time they were fighting for their lives.

'I want to have another go at the radio,' Mike said, after they had rested for a few minutes. 'There might be another chance of getting through.'

He took out the radio and the tools and set to work. Sam watched him fiddling with the screwdriver and listened to the wash of static without much hope, but then he suddenly sat bolt upright as a voice came through clearly.

'. . . shipping in the area of Tangaroa. Due to severe volcanic activity the waters round this island are unsafe. I repeat . . .'

'Bingo!' said Mike.

'But how do we send a message?' Sam asked.

'Hang on, it's OK.'

The voice had begun speaking in French; Sam thought it was another version of the original message.

'"Severe volcanic activity",' said Jo. 'I'd never have guessed if they hadn't told me. I wonder why they need to send a warning. You'd think people would be able to see it for themselves.'

Sam shrugged. 'I suppose they have to.' Jo had reminded him that his mum, and Jo and Mike's parents, probably knew what was happening by now. They would be frantic, but they would surely have alerted the rescue services when the helicopter didn't return.

He made himself pay attention to what Mike was doing. He had found the channel to transmit, and was saying excitedly, 'Hello? Hello? Are you there? Can you hear me? Over.'

No reply.

'Can you hear me? Mayday. Mayday. We're trapped on Tangaroa. We need help. Can you hear me? Over.'

This time Sam thought he heard the

beginnings of a reply, but a powerful roar of static drowned it out and, however hard Mike tried, he couldn't make contact again.

'Never mind,' said Russ. 'You got through. I'm sure you did.'

Mike poked miserably at the innards of the radio. 'Maybe the eruption is messing up reception,' he said. 'I'll give it another go –'

'No, we'd better press on,' Russ said.

'Dad's right,' Sam said to Mike. Ash was starting to heap up outside their shelter, and he was afraid of being trapped there. 'You can try again later. Maybe the air will be clearer by then.'

He helped Mike fit the radio back inside the backpack; Jo took it from him and fastened up the straps. 'I'll carry it for a bit.'

Sam wasn't sorry to get rid of the weight. He hauled himself to his feet and peered out, past the overhanging rock. The rain of ash continued; the sky overhead was still dark. From the direction of the cone a dull-red glow lit up the sky, and over to the left was a patch of brighter red, as if trees and bushes were blazing.

'Good thing that's no closer,' Russ said, and Sam grunted agreement.

Jo took the lead down the gully away from the cone. Falling into step behind her, Sam realized she must be even more exhausted than he was, after her ordeal in the mud. She wasn't moaning about it, though; she could obviously take it. Sam grinned. He'd thought Jo was really ditzy at first; how wrong could you be about anybody?

Mike wasn't doing too badly, either. He was scared, but fixing the radio had helped him take his mind off the situation and had given him a reason to be pleased with himself. He'd come through, too. They all would, Sam was sure.

Just as he came to this comforting conclusion, Sam realized that his dad, who was bringing up the rear, had stopped and was dropping behind. 'Jo, hang on!' he called. He turned round, trying to make out his dad's figure through the rain of ash. 'Dad, not more pictures, for –'

He broke off as he saw that Russ was looking upwards, staring and then beginning to fumble for his camera. Above them, along with the ash and smoke, a fountain of orange fire was blasting out of the top of Tangaroa.

The very lip of the cone was outlined in a

brilliant band, almost as if the sun was rising out of the volcano. As Sam watched, the band became a wave, surging over the rim and beginning to run down the slopes like fizzy drink overflowing from a bottle. Below, red seams opened up as the skin of the dome cracked and more fire poured out.

He felt Jo grab his arm. 'Lava!' she shouted. 'It's molten lava!'

CHAPTER SEVEN

Mike was standing beside his sister, staring up at the lava as it poured down the side of the cone in streams of fire. 'It'll catch us!' he said. 'We'll be burnt.'

Sam thought Mike was going to start crying, or maybe lose his head completely and give way to panic. 'No,' he said firmly. 'It's coming slowly. Look. We can keep ahead of it.'

Mike looked uncertain, but Jo added, 'Sam's right. And by the time it gets this far, it'll slow down even more. It might not get here at all. Isn't that right, Sam?'

'Right,' said Sam. 'All the same, let's get going. Dad, have you finished?'

His father had already tucked the camera back in the bag and started down the gully to catch them up. 'Right with you, Sam,' he said.

As they moved off again, Sam couldn't help wondering whether any of the pictures his dad was taking would ever come out. What would the heat and ash do to the camera and the film? But he could understand why Russ had to try. Maybe the camera was his way of dealing with the danger, just as the radio was Mike's.

Photography wasn't just his dad's job. It was something Russ *had* to do. That might mean, Sam reflected, that there would be times when somebody else had to take the practical decisions. Like me, now. And I'd better get it right.

The gully led almost straight downwards, the slope becoming steeper. The ash was beginning to fill up the uneven places, so it was harder to see where to put their feet. Gradually their pace slowed as they realized it would be easy to slip. Any serious injury now would severely reduce their chances of survival.

Even while he was trying to tread

carefully, Sam couldn't help glancing over his shoulder from time to time at the lava flow behind them. The searing orange fire covered all the upper part of the volcano that he could see; Tangaroa was a cone of flame. Sam could hardly believe that it wasn't actually flame at all, but rock – rock hot enough to flow like water. If they couldn't move fast enough, it would engulf them and, unlike the mud, this time there would be no escape.

But for the time being they were well ahead. Sam even thought that the air was growing cooler, and the ash fall was not quite so thick, as if they were moving away from the worst of it. He was beginning to find it easier to breathe.

But he barely had time to feel optimistic, or to say something encouraging to the others. 'I reckon we're –' he began, then broke off as Jo, trudging just ahead of him, came to an abrupt stop.

'No! I don't believe it!' he heard her say. She sounded furious.

Sam pushed ahead to join her, and she flung an arm out, keeping him back. 'Stop,' she said. 'Don't come any further. Look.'

Sam looked where she was pointing. A metre or so ahead of her, the rock walls came to an end. The path they were following broke off. They were standing on the edge of a precipice.

Moments later, Mike and Russ came to a halt behind them. 'What's wrong?' Mike asked.

Jo slipped off the backpack and let it fall at the side of the path. Wriggling her shoulders to ease her muscles, she said, 'We just ran out of road.'

Sam was already moving forward cautiously so that he could lie flat on the edge and see if there was a way down. Directly in front of him the rock face plunged straight down until it disappeared into foliage about ten metres below – bushes or the tops of trees, Sam could not tell in the poor light. To left and right, the path curved round the rock face and became a narrow ledge. On the right it vanished after a few metres, but on the left it seemed to go on indefinitely, or at least as far as Sam could see.

He pushed himself backwards, away from the drop, until he felt safe enough to sit up.

Jo and Russ were both examining the rock walls on either side. 'I don't fancy trying to climb that,' Russ said.

'Well, we can't go back,' Jo said.

'We'll run into the lava if we go back,' Mike pointed out.

Russ came to join Sam and looked over the precipice as he had done. 'That ledge,' he said, pointing to the left-hand route. 'It might be the only way out.'

'If you're a fly,' Sam said.

'No, look,' Russ insisted. 'It's not as narrow as it looks – no different from a pavement back home. It's just the drop that makes it look bad.'

'Oh, that's all right, then,' said Jo sarcastically.

Sam looked again at the ledge. Maybe his dad was right. In any case, it was a choice between that and going back up the gully to meet the lava on its way down. 'Well, OK, let's give it a go,' he said.

'I'll go first,' said Russ. 'Mike, you're next, then Jo, and, Sam, you keep a lookout behind.'

Carefully he moved out on to the ledge, steadying himself with one hand against the rock wall.

Mike hesitated.

'Go on, Mike,' Jo said. 'You'll be fine. Just don't look down.'

Nervously, Mike began edging along after Russ, keeping his face turned towards the rock. Jo went next, looking as calm as if she was strolling down to the shops. Sam picked up the backpack, took a last look up into the dark hollow of the gully, and followed her.

The ledge was about a metre wide, and fairly flat. After he had been moving along it for a minute or so, Sam could see what his dad meant. He wasn't going to fall, unless he deliberately went too close to the edge. All that worried him was that it didn't seem to be going down.

After a while, the ledge curved sharply round a jutting rock. Sam saw his dad disappear round it and almost at once heard a loud exclamation. 'What's the matter?' he shouted.

'Come and look!'

Sam crowded up behind the others. When he rounded the bend, he could see what the trouble was. The ledge came to an abrupt end where the precipice had fallen away into broken rock and scree. Russ was staring at it with an exasperated look.

'Will we have to go back?' Mike asked.

And what then? Sam thought.

He squatted down so that he could look more closely. 'Hang on a minute. Maybe we can get down.' Where the ledge ended was a mass of huge boulders which quickly gave way to smaller rocks and pebbles. Sam didn't dare put his feet down; he could imagine them giving way, letting him slide down – into what? The bushes at the bottom of the gully had disappeared into darkness now. There was nothing to show whether the slope went on for a few metres or a few hundred.

'I wish we had a torch,' Jo said.

'Yes,' Mike agreed. 'I'd give anything for my flashlight.'

'Flash!' said Sam. 'Dad, your flash gun! Is it powerful enough to show us what's down there?'

'Brilliant!' Russ was already fiddling with the camera. 'All ready? Keep your eyes peeled; it won't last long. OK – one, two, three . . .'

The slope was lit up by a flash of brilliant

light. Sam tried to force his eyes to stay open but he blinked automatically, screwing up his eyes. However, he had seen what they needed to know: the scree came to an end about twenty metres below, in a tumble of rocks and bushes. It looked as if there was a way down.

Jo gave Sam a sideways grin. 'Going to eat the camera, then? You said you would if it was any use!'

Sam swatted at her amiably.

'I'll go first,' Russ said, stowing the camera away in the bag.

'No,' said Sam. He wasn't used to arguing with his dad, but this time he felt he had to. 'Dad, if . . . if there's a problem down there, it's best if you stay with Jo and Mike. I'll go.'

Russ looked at him for a minute, weighing him up. 'OK,' he said eventually.

Sam knew he was taking a risk. If this was a dead end, or if there was something nasty lurking down there that they couldn't see, then he probably wouldn't be able to climb back up again. 'When I shout, you come after me, OK?' he said.

Russ grinned at him. 'Yessir. Right away, sir.'

Sam handed the backpack to Russ then scrambled over the boulders and climbed down carefully on to the scree. The small stones shifted under his feet, and suddenly he was sliding, picking up speed as clouds of ash boiled up around him. He heard stones crunching and pattering, and then he let out a yell as he slammed into a tangle of branches and something sharp drove into his hand.

Russ's voice came down from the ledge. 'Sam? Are you OK?'

'Fine!' Sam shouted back. 'Just had a fight with a bush, that's all. Six-inch thorns.'

He scrambled clear, pulled the thorn out and sucked the heel of his hand as he peered around through the ash. He had ended up in a thicket of spiky bushes and rock at the bottom of the slope, on a wide semi-circle of volcanic rock. On all sides, except the direction he had come from, were more cliffs, broken and uneven, falling away once again into darkness. There was no obvious way to go on, but anything was better than going back to face the lava.

'OK!' he shouted. 'Come on!'

From the darkness above came the sound of more loose stones, and then Mike shot into view, sitting on the loose scree as if he was sledging. Sam caught him before he hit the bushes. Jo followed, and a minute later Russ brought up the rear, hugging the camera bag and backpack.

'Which way now?' Jo asked as she got to her feet.

'Let's take a look,' said Russ. 'Shout if you see anything promising.'

While Jo and Mike made for the edge of the cliffs to look for a way down, Sam stood and gazed back at the cone of Tangaroa. The molten lava was still pouring out of it, cloaking the mountain in flame. He thought the blast of ash and rock was growing less strong; the roaring was certainly not as loud. He wondered uneasily where the lava was heading, and how close to them it was. If they were lucky, it could flow down the other side of the mountain and never reach them at all, but, after all that had happened that day, he didn't feel like relying on luck.

Just as he was about to move off, he heard a sudden clatter of rock, and a scream. 'Jo! Sam! Help!'

It was Mike's voice. Sam looked round wildly, but he couldn't see the younger boy anywhere. 'Mike!' he shouted. 'Mike, where are you?'

Jo dashed up to him. 'Mike! Mike!'

For a horrible few seconds there was silence, and then Mike's voice came again. 'I'm here – the rock gave way! Help me, somebody! I can't hold on!'

CHAPTER EIGHT

'**I**'m coming!' Sam sprinted towards the sound, with Jo at his heels. 'Hang on, Mike! I'm coming!'

Russ was hurrying across from the other side of the semi-circle, slowed down by loose rock. Sam halted near the edge and looked from side to side. 'Mike, keep shouting! I can't see you!'

'Here! I'm slipping . . . Help!'

Sam looked down to see Mike clinging a metre or so below the edge of the cliff. The fingers of one hand were locked round a projecting stone, while the other hand scrabbled for a grip. His face was white, his eyes wide with terror.

Jo knelt and reached for him, but Sam pushed her aside. 'Let me. I've got a longer reach.'

For a second Jo looked as if she wanted to argue, but then she moved back so that Sam could stretch out on the ground and hold out a hand to Mike. Mike grabbed it. Suddenly Sam found he was taking most of the boy's weight. The rock under him shifted. Keeping his voice calm, he said to Mike, 'Can you find a foothold?'

'No. Sam, don't let go!'

'It's OK.'

Reaching down, he managed to grip Mike's other wrist. He realized his dad was crouching beside him and he muttered, 'Keep back, Dad. The rock's going to give way.' He hoped Mike couldn't hear.

He could feel it shifting again, under his chest where he hung over the cliff. Beyond Mike's scared face, he could see nothing but darkness.

He began wriggling backwards, trying to pull Mike up, but he was too far forward to get a proper hold and, as he moved, the backpack, which he had been carrying over one shoulder, slewed round to the front and slipped over the edge, nearly pulling Sam with it.

Mike screamed. Sam felt hands grip his ankles, and heard his dad's voice saying, 'OK, I've got you.'

Sam and Mike were still swaying dangerously over the cliff. Sam felt as if his arms were being wrenched out of their sockets.

'Hold on! I need to get rid of this bag. I'm going to let go of one hand for just a second. Don't panic!' Carefully he let go of one of Mike's hands, and the strap of the backpack slid down his arm until the pack came free and dropped out of sight. It seemed a long time before Sam heard it crash down below.

Free of the extra weight, it was easier for Russ to pull Sam back. After a few minutes' frantic scrabbling, Sam hauled Mike over the edge and back out of danger. A few chunks of loose rock pattered and bounded into the depths.

Mike huddled on the ground, shivering, and Jo put her arms round him. She looked up at Sam and his dad. 'Thanks, fellas.'

Russ patted her shoulder. 'Take a rest,' he said. 'Sam and I will look for a way down.'

Sam flexed his arms: his muscles were painful after the strain. His arms and legs had been scraped from being dragged across the rock, and he was shaking as he thought about falling into the dark. But he was all in one piece, and so was Mike. 'We lost the radio,' he said.

'And that last can of drink,' Jo said regretfully. 'I wish we'd had it before.'

'Too bad.' Sam shrugged. 'Anyway, we probably got through. There could be a rescue boat on the way already.'

He wasn't sure if he believed that, but there was no point in worrying. All they could do now was get down to the beach so that they stood a chance of being seen.

He was still thinking about it when he heard a shout from his dad, who had gone back to the other side of the plateau. He was waving. 'There's a path!' he called. 'Come and look.'

Jo helped Mike to his feet. 'Let's go.'

'Thanks, Sam,' Mike said. He'd been crying and ash was smeared over his face – but he looked better now and fit to carry on.

'I'm really sorry about the radio. It's my fault we lost it.'

'No it wasn't, it was an accident,' Sam said, as they picked their way over the stony ground towards his dad. 'Anyway, without you it wouldn't have worked at all.' Mike looked a bit more cheerful. 'And at least we don't have to carry it any more.'

Russ was standing at the top of a rocky path that led steeply downwards through the bushes. The going looked much easier than anything they had faced so far, and Sam couldn't help feeling more hopeful as his dad led the way down. Previously, the cliffs had held them up but, now they were on the move again, they might be able to outpace the lava.

It felt hotter, and Sam thought he could hear a crackling behind him, as if trees and shrubs were catching fire, but when he glanced back he could see nothing. He also heard rustling in the undergrowth, and once he caught sight of a small brown shape darting across the path. The animals of Tangaroa were fleeing from the volcano too.

At last the path started to level out. They crossed another wide plateau, this time carpeted with thick vegetation. Sam hoped that any lurking snakes had other things on their mind than biting people.

Beyond the plateau was a line of trees; beyond that, everything was dark. Sam groaned at the thought of another precipice. But as he drew closer to the trees, he could hear another sound: the steady swell and crash of waves breaking against land.

'The beach!' Jo cried.

'We're there!' said Mike.

They broke through the barrier of trees, and stood staring out to sea. They hadn't reached the beach; they were standing on a high cliff above it. A hot wind lashed the trees. In front of them the sky churned with dark clouds, but there was enough light to make out the sea below.

Where, earlier, blue waves had rolled gently on to the shore, the sea was now grey and angry. Huge waves were battering the coast, throwing spray high into the air. Sam drew in his breath. It was magnificent, but it was terrifying too.

Jo sniffed. 'Pity I forgot my surfboard.'

'Now that would be a great picture.' Russ grinned wearily at her. 'I'd give a lot for that.'

Of course, he was pulling the camera out again; Sam decided against saying something rude. He was just thankful for the chance to have a rest. He glanced at his watch, only to find that it was broken – when he hit the bottom of the slope, he supposed. His stomach was telling him it was a long way past lunchtime.

'Why is it so rough?' Mike asked. 'Has there been a storm as well?'

'It's something you get with volcanoes,' Russ said, squinting through the viewfinder. 'Sometimes a real tidal wave, but this doesn't look quite so bad.'

'I can't see any beach left at all,' said Jo. 'The water's much higher than it was.'

'And there's no rescue boat,' Mike added.

'Give them time,' Russ said encouragingly. 'I know it seems like we've been here for ever, but it's not really all that long.'

Getting down to the water's edge was still their best chance of safety; nobody could argue with that. But it didn't look as safe as they'd all hoped. Sam let out a huge sigh. Was everything they did bound to go wrong?

Waiting for his dad to finish fiddling with

the camera, Sam turned to look back through the trees. What he saw made him reach out blindly, grabbing Jo who was next to him. 'Look!'

Further up the mountain, in the direction they had come, lava was beginning to cascade over a precipice. Sam guessed it was the ledge they had been walking along not long before. When he first saw it, it was no more than a few fiery trickles, but it rapidly grew and spread, pouring down until the whole of the cliff was a curtain of flame. At the foot of the rocks, trees and bushes blazed up. A hot wind brought the sound of crackling to them, drowning out the crashing of the waves below.

For a minute Sam couldn't do anything but stand and stare. Part of him was terrified, and part of him thought he'd never seen anything so magnificent.

'It's going to catch us!' Mike exclaimed.

'Not if we're quick,' said Sam, snapping out of his brief stupor. 'Dad, come on.'

Russ had put the camera away and was already heading for the edge of the cliff, looking for a way down. The others followed. On the seaward side, the land fell away gradually into a shallow valley. Sam guessed there might have been a stream at the bottom, though now everything was choked with the volcanic ash. At least the going looked easier.

They set off at a good pace. Sam glanced over his shoulder at the pouring lava, found his feet sinking unexpectedly into hot ash, staggered downwards, and was saved from falling only when he cannoned into Jo. 'Sorry,' he gasped.

'Don't worry,' she said, clutching at him to keep her own balance. 'Watch where you're putting your feet, huh?'

Sam realized that the slope, which had looked so easy, was filled with holes and hummocks, smoothed out and covered by the ash. He called out to his dad and Mike, who had drawn ahead, 'Be careful, there's –' then he broke off as he saw Russ slip sideways and crash to the ground, falling awkwardly as he tried to save the camera bag. 'Dad!' Sam yelled.

By the time he reached his father's side, Russ was trying to get up. Mike was bent over him, looking worried.

'Dad, are you OK?' Sam asked.

'Fine.' The word was a gasp of pain. Russ bit his lower lip, almost managed to stand, then slipped back into the ash.

Sam knelt beside his dad and helped him to sit up. Russ's breath hissed through his teeth as he tried to move.

'Have you broken something?' Sam asked anxiously.

'Don't think so. Give me a hand.'

Hanging on to Sam, Russ struggled to his feet, though Sam wasn't at all sure that he was going to stay there. He was trying to balance on his right leg, as if the left one was too painful to put his weight on. His hands had plunged into the ash in an effort to break his fall, and now they looked reddened as if they were burnt. Sam wished they hadn't lost the first-aid kit along with the radio and the other stuff in the backpack.

Russ swayed as Sam held on to his arm. 'OK.' His voice was tight. 'Let's go.' He took one step, lurching when he had to stand on the injured leg, then another. Jo went to pick up the camera bag, and he shook his head. 'No – too much weight. Leave it.'

More than anything else, that convinced Sam that his dad was badly hurt. He would rather cut off his hand than abandon his photographic gear.

'Just bring the camera,' Russ said. 'I'll save the pictures I've taken if it's the last thing I do.'

Jo passed the strap of the camera round her own neck, and led the way to the bottom of the slope. After the first few paces, Russ seemed to manage better. He wasn't putting all his weight on Sam, though Sam still kept hold of his arm to steady him.

He was aware now of how slowly they were going. The lava must be gaining on them. Partly it was Russ's injury, partly that they were all so tired. It felt as if they had been climbing and stumbling down this mountain for a lifetime, and they still seemed no closer to safety.

At the foot of the slope was a morass of ash and mud, as the choked-up stream overflowed its banks and tried to find a channel.

'Let's follow it down,' Jo said. 'That has to be the quickest way to the sea.'

'Good idea,' said Sam.

'Mike, you go first,' Jo instructed. 'Don't wait for us, just keep your eyes open, and yell if you see anything we need to know.'

Mike gave her a frightened look but he didn't say anything, only turned and started to make his way along the bed of the stream, squelching through the mud.

'It's looking bad, isn't it?' Jo said softly when he had drawn some way ahead.

'Not good,' Russ agreed.

'Sam, do you think we can get to the beach ahead of the lava?'

Sam wondered why she was asking him. Then he started to realize that, with his dad hurt, there was nobody else she could ask. He was their leader now, whether he liked it or not. 'Yes, I do,' he said determinedly. 'I'm not giving in, not now we've come so far.'

His dad grinned at him; it was all he could do to keep putting one foot in front of the other, without saying anything.

Jo wiped a hand across her forehead. 'I've had it with this,' she said. 'Heat and ash and mud. I've had it up to here. And what do we do when we get to the beach, that's what I want to know.'

Sam had been wondering that, too. What if the lava drove them into the sea? How long would they be able to last out? Surprising himself by how confident he sounded, he said, 'We'll worry about that when we get there.'

'There'd better be a boat, that's all,' said Jo.

'There will be.'

Jo didn't argue. 'Mike worries me,' she admitted after a minute. 'When Mum said we could come, she told me to look after him.'

'Well, she can hardly blame you for this,' said Sam.

'Mike's a good kid,' said Russ.

Sam watched Mike's small figure for a while; he was still in sight, though some way ahead now, and further downstream. Several times he slipped, nearly losing his footing, but he kept going. Occasionally he glanced back at the others to make sure they were still following.

'Why don't you catch up with him and make sure he's OK?' Sam suggested. 'Dad and I are doing fine.'

'Sure,' said Jo. She flashed a grin. 'I'll tell him –'

She broke off. Mike had turned to face them and he was waving his hands above his head. Sam could hear him shouting. 'Jo! Sam! Come here! Come quick!'

Jo and Sam exchanged a startled glance.

'Go on,' said Sam. 'See what he wants. We'll be right behind you.'

Jo hurried on ahead at once. Sam followed more slowly, still helping Russ. When Jo caught up with Mike, he grabbed her, pointing at something away to the left. It was a few minutes more before Sam and Russ came close enough to see what it was.

Where Mike and Jo were standing the ground had flattened out, and they could see further than before. A hundred metres or so away, a tongue of lava was creeping through the trees. The leading edge was bright flame, setting fire to the grass and shrubs in its path, while on top and just behind, the bright orange fire was fading to grey and then to dull black as the lava solidified to rock.

The crackling of the fire was louder now. Sam could see hundreds of small animals hopping through the grass, away from the fire. Some streaked ahead of it, scurrying into the shelter of the untouched foliage. From a distance they heard the thin shriek of a creature that had not fled fast enough.

'We'll never get away!' Mike started to sob.

'Stop it!' Jo said forcefully. She put an arm round his shoulders.

'No, Mike, look,' Sam said. 'It's not coming this way. We've just got to keep going.'

Mike gulped, thrust his fists into his eyes, and took a deep breath. 'OK,' he said. 'But let's just *go*, please.'

'This way, then,' Sam said, pointing along the stream bed. 'It keeps on going down.'

Mike went first again, sliding and stumbling through the ash and mud; Jo followed him, and Sam brought up the rear with Russ.

As they tried to hurry, Sam kept an eye on the lava flow to their left. More fires were breaking out as the lava poured down, reaching out for the sea like the fingers of a huge hand. To his relief, it didn't come any closer to where they were, and the mountainside to their right remained dark.

We're not cut off yet, Sam thought to himself. And, with luck, we never will be.

Then he thought he heard a shout. At first he assumed it came from Jo or Mike, but they were struggling on, just ahead of him. Besides, the shout had sounded as if it came from further away.

Sam assumed he had imagined it, or it had been the cry of some animal, distorted by the roaring of the fire. Then it came again.

He halted. 'Dad, did you hear that?'

'What?' Russ looked too dazed with pain to have noticed anything.

'I thought – there!'

The shout came again, and through the leaping flames Sam could see a dark shape. At first he couldn't believe what was in front of his eyes. Not an animal, but someone staggering upright, arms round his head to shield it from the fire. The figure appeared from behind a bank of flame where a clump of bushes was blazing. Sam recognized him, and at the same moment Jo grabbed his arm.

'Sam!' she cried. 'It's Zack!'

CHAPTER NINE

Sam thought that Zack didn't realize they were there: he was blundering to and fro as if he didn't know which way to go, or how to save himself from the molten lava.

'Zack!' Sam yelled. 'Here – over here!'

Zack seemed not to hear him. He began staggering off in the opposite direction, then he tripped over something and fell. For a moment he struggled to get up again, then he lay still.

Jo sucked in a breath that sounded like a sob. 'He's going to die!'

Sam knew he couldn't just stand there and watch, or carry on as if he didn't know that

Zack was there. He had to do something, even though the delay meant more danger.

'Listen, Dad,' he said, 'you rest for a minute.' He guided Russ over to a rock where he could sit. Russ obeyed him without protest and sat, slumped, with his head down. Sam couldn't ever remember seeing him when he wasn't a bundle of energy, but his injured leg had obviously drained all his strength. 'I'm going to see if I can get across to Zack,' he went on. 'If you two want to carry on, we can catch you up later.'

'No,' Jo said immediately. 'We'll stick together. If we lose each other, we've had it.' Hesitating, with a glance at Mike, she added, 'You know this is going to finish us, don't you? If the lava doesn't catch up with us, how do you think you're going to get Zack and your dad down to the beach?'

Sam shrugged. 'Zack can walk.'

He looked back across the lava flow to where Zack had managed to get to his feet and was staggering away from them, heading down the slope but towards the next stream of fire.

'Just,' said Jo.

'He'll die if we leave him,' Mike said. The younger boy was looking terrified, but Sam was surprised how well he was controlling his fear.

Sam cupped his hands round his mouth and yelled the pilot's name several times, but either the roar of the fire drowned out his voice, or Zack was too stupefied to hear. 'I can't just walk away from him,' he said to Jo.

Jo gave him a despairing look, but all she said was, 'I know. Let's just get on with it, huh?'

Sam pulled himself out of the bed of the stream and looked around. Now on slightly higher ground, he could see more clearly what was going on. Several streams of lava were snaking their way across the mountainside, solidifying as they went. On either side of them, trees and bushes blazed like torches, and the fire was gradually spreading to fill the spaces between. The narrow wedges of clear ground were slowly being engulfed.

Sam knew he had only a few minutes to reach Zack before they would both be trapped. But a river of lava flowed between them. He took a few paces forward, shielding his eyes from the glare and heat, and knowing that it would be suicide to try to cross. Maybe it was already too late for Zack.

'I'm not giving in,' he muttered through clenched teeth.

He followed the lava downwards for a few metres, but the leading edge was out of sight; there was no obvious way of getting round it. Sam retraced his steps, staring in frustration at the glowing surface as it gradually cooled and darkened and solidified.

Solidified . . . the word went through his mind. On the near side of the flow the mud from the stream had damped down the fire; what there was burned sluggishly, with more smoke than flame. Sam chose a spot where he could get close to the lava flow itself, grabbed a stick and poked at the crust on top, but it quickly broke; Sam dropped the stick as it dipped into the molten rock and caught fire.

There was no hope that such a thin crust of rock could support his weight. At least . . . 'Not here,' he said aloud. 'But maybe further up . . .'

'What are you muttering about?' Jo asked.

'I'm going back up the flow,' Sam explained. 'Up there, where it's cooler, I can maybe get across it.'

Jo stared at him, open-mouthed. 'Sam Carlsen, you are totally out of your tree!'

'Maybe, but I've got to try. Zack saved us when he made us get out of the 'copter first.' He glanced across to where Zack lay, huddled on the ground again, surrounded by sheets of flame. 'It's his only chance.'

Jo took in a long breath. 'I'll come with you,' she said.

'No.' Sam reached out and gripped her arm. 'Look, Jo, if – well, if it goes wrong, do your best for Dad and Mike, OK?'

'OK.'

Sam smiled at her and started to climb. After the first few paces he began to draw away from the worst of the fire, as the vegetation was burning itself out. The lava flow looked like a solid river of rock, though Sam was not deceived. He knew that it was hiding a fiery, molten core.

Before very long, he came to a place where the lava flow was clear of flames on both sides; Sam could see across to the smouldering, blackened land the fire had left behind it. The surface of the lava flow was black, and twisted like a hank of thick rope.

He found another stick and poked cautiously at the surface; this time, even when he prodded hard, he could not break through the crust. He glanced back to where he could still see Jo beside his dad, and muttered, 'It's now or never.'

Very carefully, he stepped up on to the surface of the lava, and let it take his weight, ready to jump back if he felt it start to give way. It held, but there was a spongy feeling under his feet, as if the rock was very gradually sinking.

His stomach lurched. Instead of jumping back, he ran forward, fast and light, so his feet had as little contact with the surface as possible. Within moments he was stumbling down into the ash of the fire on the far side.

He was across.

Feeling encouraged, he set off towards the spot where he had last seen the pilot.

Walking over the hot ash was almost worse than running across the lava. Sam could feel the heat striking up through the soles of his trainers. The ash he stirred up settled on him and stung. Now he had to find a path through blazing trees, and he was afraid of being cut off himself. Shielding his eyes against the glare, he plodded forward as if he was trying to push through a solid wall of heat, until he again caught sight of the dark shape that was Zack.

The pilot was still stumbling downwards, but to Sam's eyes he looked exhausted. He kept falling and having to struggle to get up again.

'Zack! Zack!' Sam yelled again.

This time the pilot heard him. He turned, peering through the flames. Sam hurried towards him, dodging around the burning shrubs and creeping flame that flowed through the undergrowth. As he reached the more open ground where Zack was, he called out again; Zack saw him. He had a cut across his eye and his hair and clothes were pitted with dirt.

'It's OK, Zack,' Sam said, panting. 'We're all here. We'll get you to the beach. There'll be a boat –'

Zack was not listening. His eyes were wild and frightened. As Sam started to speak, he let out a long howl. Then, as Sam started towards him, he picked up a blazing branch from the floor and staggered forward, sweeping it around like a weapon.

'Zack!' Sam said, stepping back. 'What's with you? Listen –'

The branch traced a vicious curve just in front of Sam. It shed blazing leaves into the air and Sam had to bat them away with his hands.

'Get away!' the pilot yelled. 'You left me! You left me up there to die!'

CHAPTER TEN

'You've got it all wrong!' Sam gasped out. 'Wait!'

The pilot took no notice. He lurched forward, still trying to swat Sam with the blazing branch. Sam ducked underneath it and sidestepped out of range.

'Sam!' It was Jo's voice. She had seen what was happening and was calling out to him from the other side of the lava flow. 'Sam, I'm coming over!'

'No!' Sam shouted back. He was angry. It was bad enough having to dodge Zack, without the bother of dealing with Jo as well, even though he knew she meant to help. 'Too dangerous – I can deal with it! Stay clear, OK?'

'But Sam, he's going to –'

Sam tuned her out. Zack was swivelling round, getting ready to lash at him again. The undergrowth all round them was blazing up; if they didn't get a move on, Sam knew, they would be cut off by the fire.

'Give up, will you?' he shouted.

The pilot ran at him, but before he could reach Sam he tripped over something and pitched forward, losing his grip of the branch. He yelled with pain as his hands hit the hot earth.

Sam darted in from the side, grabbed Zack's shoulders and heaved him upright. His breath sobbed in the scalding air as he dragged the man away from the worst of the fire.

Flames were licking over the pilot's torn jacket. Sam managed to reach a clear space that was so far untouched by the fire, and rolled him over on the ground, putting the flames out. The pilot lay still.

Sam stood over him for a few seconds, taking in great gulps of air. Then, still aware of the fire heading towards them, he took the man by his shoulders again and started to drag him.

'Sam?' It was Jo again. 'Sam, are you OK?'

No, Sam thought. I'm worn out and scared out of my wits. 'Yes, fine!' he called back.

'What do you want me to do?'

Sam thought fast. He wasn't sure he could get Zack back up the slope and through the fire. Their only hope was to keep going down the mountainside towards the sea.

'Take Dad,' he told Jo. 'Get hold of Mike and carry on down. We'll meet on the beach,' he said, gesturing frantically down the slope.

He didn't have time to see whether she obeyed his instructions. The fire was coming on too fast. He started dragging Zack again, unsure that they would be able to stay in front of it. 'I'm not leaving you now,' he said through clenched teeth. 'Not even if you did try to kill me.'

To his relief, after a few minutes the pilot stirred, then he started muttering and struggling against Sam's grip. Sam hauled him to his feet and pushed him ahead in the direction they had to go. At first he thought

Zack would fall over again, but he managed to keep going and only needed Sam to steady him or steer him.

For a few minutes they made better time, and managed to outdistance the worst of the flames, but as Sam glanced over his shoulder he saw that more of the lava was pouring down the slope behind them, a fiery line creeping over the ground and drawing gradually closer.

At that very moment Zack stumbled. Sam rushed forward to help him stand up again and soon found that he was taking most of his weight. He pulled the man's arm over his shoulders; Zack moaned with pain but did not resist as Sam half carried him onwards.

Just when Sam was beginning to feel that he couldn't go another step, he heard Jo shouting his name.

Then she was beside him, taking some of Zack's weight so that they could go faster.

'I told you to stay clear,' Sam mumbled.

'I did. It's OK, Sam. It's better up ahead. You'll see.'

Sam couldn't believe that anything could be better on this horrible mountain, but Jo was right. After a few minutes they arrived back at the choked-up stream bed and reached a place where the lava was splashing down into a deep pit that might once have been a pool at the foot of a waterfall. It was easy to skirt the downstream side and make for the clear area beyond it.

Mike was waiting for them there with Russ, who was slumped on the ground with his back against a rock. Sam felt really happy to see his dad again; for a few minutes back there, he'd wondered if he ever would.

Mike's blackened face was split by a wide grin. 'Sam, I've seen the sea!' he exclaimed. 'We're nearly there.'

'Mike's a good leader,' Jo said, smiling at her brother. His grin widened even more at her words of praise.

Sam let Zack slip to the ground beside his father. Mike's optimism revived him, though he wasn't sure he shared it. He couldn't see how three youngsters could get two injured men down to the beach or what they would do once they were there.

Take it a step at a time, he said to himself. We've come this far.

The pilot kept wiping one hand over his face and muttering to himself. Sam squatted down beside him. 'I'm sorry we left you up there,' he said. 'We looked for you, honest. We thought you were dead.'

Zack gave him a bleary stare. Sam guessed that the pilot didn't remember attacking him, and he didn't mean to remind him. Getting a better look at him, he could see that his jacket and shirt were burnt; the shirt was sticking to his body, as if the flesh underneath was burnt as well. His face and neck and hands were reddened, and some of the skin was peeling. Dried blood matted his hair and spread down one side of his face from the cut over his eye. Sam wished they still had the first-aid kit, and then realized that first aid wouldn't do Zack much good; what he needed was a hospital, and fast.

'What happened?' Sam asked.

Zack rubbed his hand over his face again.

'Got out when we crashed,' he muttered. 'Head was hurting. Tried to climb, and then I fell. Don't remember . . . When I woke up, it was burning, all burning.'

He fell silent and turned his head away.

Sam tried to make sense of it. Zack had probably climbed the ridge as soon as he got out of the helicopter, and had lost consciousness from his head injury. He must have been lying somewhere among the lush vegetation in the valley, perhaps not far away from where Sam and Russ had searched for him.

'We should get on,' Jo said.

'Slave-driver,' Russ said, beginning to heave himself to his feet.

Sam shook Zack gently. 'Come on. We've got to get down to the beach.'

Zack shrugged his hand away and didn't move. 'Can't. Gotta rest.'

'Rest later,' Sam said.

With Jo's help he managed to haul the pilot upright and propel him forward. Russ was managing to walk by himself, though Mike stayed beside him and steadied him over the rougher patches of ground.

They were heading away from the lava and the fire, which faded to a dull red glow behind them. The air felt cooler on Sam's sweating face, and he could smell the sea. Mike must have been right: they were close to the beach.

What then? Sam asked himself. Would they be able to rest, or would the lava flow all the way down to the beach and force them out into the sea? How long could they stay afloat if it did?

Suddenly Mike darted forward. Ahead, the slope seemed to come to an abrupt end, and for a minute Sam thought he was going to spring off into empty air. Instead he stopped on the very edge and turned back. 'Look! It's the sea!'

The others caught up with him, and they all stood on the edge of the bluff, gazing out to sea. It was calmer now; the big waves they had seen from higher up the mountain had given way to a heavy swell. Sam thought he could see something dark floating on the surface, but he couldn't make out what it was.

'Jo?' He pointed. 'What do you reckon that is?'

Jo shrugged. 'Dunno. Seaweed?'

It could be, Sam thought. Stuff disturbed at the bottom of the sea and washed up on the coast. Not that it mattered, he decided. The important thing for them was to find a way down.

He was just turning away, steering Zack along, when Jo exclaimed, 'Wait!'

Sam stopped. 'What?'

'I saw something out there.'

She pointed out towards the dark horizon. Clouds covered the sky, so it was hard to see where it ended and the sea began. Sam couldn't see anything. 'It's not –' he began.

'There!'

This time Sam saw it too. A light out at sea, shining brightly for a minute and then vanishing again. As he watched, it reappeared. At first he couldn't work out why it should come and go, but then he realized that each time a wave heaved up it would come between the light and the shore.

He realized what it must be at the same time that Mike cried out, 'It's a boat! It's a rescue boat! They've come to get us!'

CHAPTER ELEVEN

Jo and Sam raised their voices in a tired cheer, and even Russ joined in. Only Zack was too far gone in pain and exhaustion to understand what was happening.

'Mike, that's great,' Sam said, clapping the younger boy on the back. 'They wouldn't be here if it wasn't for you and the radio.'

Mike beamed and straightened up, as if the praise, and the hope of rescue, had given him new energy.

'We've got to get down there,' Jo said.

'Wait a minute,' said Sam. 'There's got to be a way of signalling them. If they don't know we're here, they might just turn round and go away again.'

He had a feeling of sudden urgency as he spoke, and he knew that everyone else shared it. With safety so close, they wouldn't be able to bear it if the boat went away and left them there.

'Dad, the camera,' he said. 'Give them a burst of the flash gun.'

Jo was still carrying Russ's camera round her neck. Now she took it off and passed the strap over Russ's head. He switched on the flash gun, smiling smugly at Sam. 'Not sorry that I hung on to it now, are you?'

'OK, Dad,' Sam said, grinning. 'You win.'

The flash gun whirred softly as it powered up, and Russ pressed the switch. Sam screwed up his eyes against the brilliant blue-white flash. When his vision cleared, he saw the distant light from the boat again. Now it was blinking on and off in a regular pattern, a reply to their signal. The crew knew they were there!

'Great! They've seen us!' Mike exclaimed.

'So let's get on,' Jo said.

The ground fell away steeply at the right-hand edge of the bluff. The way to the sea was clear, but it was difficult to negotiate with Russ and Zack both injured. Russ tried to climb down, but his painful hands hampered him. Sam hated to see him like that, his teeth gritted to stop himself crying out.

Russ forced a grin. 'What wouldn't I give for a sledge!'

He sat on the slope and let himself slide downwards. Jo and Sam had to lay Zack down and manoeuvre him; he was barely conscious now and quite incapable of making his own way down. He kept moaning in pain, and Sam had to stop himself from worrying about how much they were hurting him. It was that or leave him for the lava.

At the foot of the slope was a stretch of rough ground, covered in sparse vegetation. This gradually gave way to what Sam imagined must be the black sand of the beach they had seen when they approached in the helicopter, though it was hard to tell now, because everything was covered by a glutinous mud where the earlier high tide had mixed with the volcanic ash.

Twenty metres or so ahead, the waves

were rolling in. Mike squelched across the beach to the water's edge, peering out to sea. 'I can't see the boat!'

'They won't leave us,' Jo reassured him, 'not now they know we're here. It's harder to see now we're lower down, that's all.'

Sam knew she was right, but he couldn't help staring out over the dark waves and feeling immense relief whenever he saw the boat's light glimmer briefly as the swell lifted it.

'What are they playing at?' Jo said irritably. 'Why don't they come in and pick us up?'

As she finished speaking, Mike turned away from the shoreline and shouted, 'Come and look! It's really weird!'

'What now?' Jo sighed.

She and Sam let Zack slump down on the beach to rest; Russ was already squatting there, looking exhausted. Then they plodded through the mud to see what Mike had found.

As Sam reached the water's edge, he understood what the dark patches were that he had seen from the top of the bluff. They were not seaweed. Instead, it looked as if slabs and fragments of rock were floating on the surface of the water. An untidy line of the stuff marked the high waterline.

But rock doesn't float, he thought, staring at it, stupefied.

Jo picked up a small piece and turned it over in her fingers, examining it. 'It's pumice!' she said. 'You know – the stuff you use in the bath? Look.'

She held it out to him, a small fragment of grey, porous rock.

'It must have come out of the volcano,' Sam said. 'The whole sea's covered with it. Some of those pieces are massive!'

'Sam!' Jo reached out and gripped his arm. 'Sam, that must be why the boat hasn't come inshore. They can't get through this stuff.'

Sam saw Mike's mouth drop open in sudden dismay, and he knew the younger boy must be feeling just what he felt himself. 'I wonder how long it's going to take to clear,' he said.

'For ever.' Jo sounded angry. 'There could be more of it to come. I'll bet the eruption's not over.'

As if they were all in agreement, the three

of them turned and looked up towards the cone. Tangaroa was almost hidden now against the dark sky, except for dull red streaks and billows, as more material was ejected, and the burning gold of the lava that flowed down the sides. The threatening rumble was so familiar by now that they could almost ignore it, but it gave no sign of stopping.

Sam looked out to sea again and caught a reassuring glimpse of the rescue boat's light; they wouldn't go away, but they couldn't get inshore.

'We can't stay here for ever,' he said. 'There's got to be a way –'

He broke off. On the top of the bluff, where they had first seen the boat, he saw a tell-tale glint of gold. Soon lava was pouring over the edge, down to the shore about a hundred metres further along, hissing and throwing up a cloud of steam as it hit the sea. More of it was creeping down the same way that they themselves had come.

Sam checked on his dad and Zack. The pilot was lying in a heap where Sam had left him, and Russ was sitting beside him. He had seen the lava too; he pulled himself painfully to his feet and limped down to join the others at the waterline.

'I think we should make a move,' he said.

'Move where?' Jo asked. 'Further along the beach?'

'The boat won't know where we are,' Mike said, looking frightened again.

'I'll give them another flash,' Russ suggested. He switched on the flash gun and let it power up.

'Wait till we can see their light,' said Sam. 'Then we'll know they can see ours.'

His dad nodded, raised the camera high above his head, and fired the flash gun at the same time that the boat's light reappeared on the horizon. This time there was no way to be sure that the boat had seen it.

'We'd better move further along,' Sam said, since nobody else seemed about to make a decision. 'The lava will be here in a few minutes.'

'Zack is unconscious,' said Russ.

'Then we'll carry him.' Sam wasn't sure whether he and Jo could manage that, but he was going to give it a good try. 'And when we're somewhere a bit safer, we can flash to the boat again.'

'Sam –' Jo was speaking in a dry voice that didn't sound like her at all. 'I don't think we can do that. Look over there.'

Sam swivelled to follow the direction of her pointing arm. To their right, the beach curved around gently as far as a steep bank covered with trees, a hundred metres or so away. They were standing almost at the central point of a small, semicircular bay.

As Sam watched, another stream of lava oozed along the bank and began to roll down towards the sea. The trees caught fire and blazed up like torches.

Now golden glints were appearing all along the line of the ridge above the beach, gradually flowing into each other and joining into an unbroken ring of fire. Although for the moment there were still places where it looked possible to break through, Sam was certain that it was too late for them to escape that way.

The lava was surrounding them, and the ring was growing tighter every minute.

'Sam, what are we going to do?' Mike asked. He was sounding really scared again.

Sam had to come up with a workable plan pretty fast. But his mind was blank. What if

I can't? he thought. What if this is it, after all we've been through? 'OK, we can't stay here,' he said aloud, surprised at how steady his voice sounded, 'and the boat can't get to us. So we have to get to them. We've got to swim.'

CHAPTER TWELVE

'I can't swim,' Mike said. 'Not that far.' He started to cry. 'Jo, don't leave me here.'

Jo wrapped her arms round her brother. 'We're not leaving you.' She glared at Sam over the top of Mike's head. 'We'll just have to think of something else.'

'Sam.' Russ touched him on the arm. 'Come here, I want a word.'

He moved away a few paces along the beach. Sam followed him. 'Dad, we really haven't got time for –'

'No, listen.' Russ's voice was quiet, as if he didn't want Jo to hear. 'Jo's a good swimmer; I've seen her in the pool. Between you, I'm sure you could get Mike out to the boat.'

'But what about you?' Sam said. 'Dad, you can make it too.'

Russ shook his head slightly. 'I doubt it. Not like this. Zack can't, either.'

Sam glanced back to where they had left the pilot; he still lay, inert, at the bottom of the slope. Unless they moved him within minutes the lava would roll over him.

'I'll stay with him.' Russ jerked his chin upwards, daring Sam to argue. 'Then, when you get to the boat, tell them to radio for a helicopter. If you –'

'Dad, that's crazy!' Sam interrupted. 'There isn't time. The lava –'

'I want you three to get away. That's what matters.'

'No, it's not!' Sam was furious.

'Sam. None of us would have made it this far, without you,' said Russ. 'But there comes a time when you have to accept that you've done the best you can. There are five of us, and only two strong swimmers who aren't hurt. Whichever way you look at it, it's not going to work out.'

'There's got to be a way, Dad!' Sam yelled at him. He pressed his hands over his face, trying to shut out everything except the desperate need to think quickly. In books, when you got marooned, you built a raft. But there were always convenient logs, with vines or something to fasten them together, and, most important of all, there was always time. Time was what they didn't have, so, unless some raft came floating up to them ready made –

Sam caught his breath. He looked up, feeling a grin spread wide enough to split his face. 'The pumice!' he exclaimed. 'We can float out on the pumice!'

Russ stared. 'What?'

Sam grabbed his dad's shoulders. Speaking very slowly and distinctly, he repeated, 'We can float out on the pumice.'

'Got you, Sam!' Jo's voice broke in excitedly.

Sam laughed. 'Sorry, Dad. You can't be a hero today. Help Jo get Zack down here now. Mike, you help me.'

He waded out into the water until he was waist deep. Chunks of pumice were bobbing in the waves all around him. Most of them were small enough to enclose within a fist, but there were plenty of much larger ones.

Sam grabbed one that was about the size of a cushion and shoved it towards Mike, who had followed him nervously into the sea.

'Use that,' Sam said. 'Like a float in the swimming pool. Get it?'

Mike nodded. His voice shaking, he said, 'Yes, I – I get it. I can do it.'

'Great. And Mike,' he tried to speak forcefully, 'nobody's leaving anybody behind. Either we all make it or nobody does, OK?'

Mike managed to grin. 'Yeah.'

He clutched his pumice float and splashed out of the water again to where Jo and Russ were dragging Zack down the beach. Sam couldn't help pausing for a few seconds to look at the fire that flared up now in an unbroken line all along the ridge. Blazing trees sent flames leaping high into the sky, and trickles of lava were winding their way down to the beach in more than twenty different places.

Sam turned his back on the sight and waded further out, looking for a piece of pumice that would be big enough to stay afloat under Zack's weight. After the stifling heat of the volcanic ash, the sea felt cold, and the salt water stung his cuts and burns.

He was starting to panic again until he found a suitable raft – a flat, roughly circular chunk of pumice about a metre across. He had to swim to reach it, work his way round the circumference and push it back to shore. The size made it awkward to manoeuvre, and Sam couldn't help having doubts about whether he and Jo could manage to guide it out to the boat. He pushed such thoughts aside. There wasn't any other way.

By the time Sam grounded his prize in the shallows, Jo and Russ had brought the pilot to the water's edge; he was still unconscious. Just as well, Sam thought. This way, he doesn't get to vote.

Mike and Russ managed to steady the pumice raft while Sam and Jo dragged the pilot on to it. It settled under his weight and lay on the sand, just like an ordinary rock, with the sea washing round it.

'OK, this is what we do,' said Sam. 'Jo, you and I are going to push this out to the boat. Mike, you swim beside us with your float, and you too, Dad – find yourself a float if you think you're going to need it.' He looked around at all of them, compelling their attention. 'And nobody tries to be a hero. If you need help, ask for it.'

Russ tucked his camera on the raft beside Zack, fastening the strap round the pilot's belt. 'We might need the flash again,' he explained.

'And you want your pictures,' Sam teased him.

Streams of lava were creeping down the beach by now, hissing and growing dark as they came into contact with the mud, but still crawling on with the fire hot in their heart.

'Time to go,' said Sam.

He and Jo knelt in the shallows and gave the pumice raft a push. For a brief, frightening moment Sam thought they wouldn't be able to shift it. Then it slid gradually into the deeper water until it floated free. It was lower in the water than Sam had hoped, with waves washing over the top surface and lapping against Zack's body.

Jo took him by the shoulders and turned him so that his face was clear of the water. 'We'll have to push from this side,' she said.

'Make sure he can breathe. If we're not careful, he could drown while he's lying on this thing.'

As if to show that she was right, a bigger wave broke over the raft, foaming around Zack. It roused him, and he moaned with the pain of salt water on his burns. For a second he tried to sit up, and the raft rocked alarmingly. Sam grabbed it and steadied it; Zack collapsed again, muttering, and slowly slid back into unconsciousness. 'This will be harder than I thought,' Sam muttered.

With Jo at his side, he pushed the raft out until the sea-floor shelved under his feet and he had to swim. Beside them, Mike was making good progress with his float, concentrating fiercely, and Russ was swimming beside him. As they left the beach behind, a wave lifted them and once again they saw the lights of the rescue boat.

'It's not that far out,' Jo said. 'We're going to make it.'

At first Sam thought she might be right. It wasn't too difficult to push the raft, once he got into the rhythm. Push . . . kick . . . push . . . Other pieces of pumice nudged up

against the raft and bobbed aside as Jo and
Sam thrust it forward. When Sam glanced
back at the beach, it was already a hundred
metres away, streaked with the reddish gold
and black of the lava flow. He turned
his head away, and looked out to sea and
safety.

Push . . . kick . . . push. Sam tried not to
think about how tired he was. They had all
been through too much. He was especially
worried about his dad. Russ was not using a
float; Sam guessed that the rough surface of
the pumice might be too painful with his
injured hands. He was normally a strong
swimmer, but now pain and exhaustion were
making his movements laboured.

Their progress was incredibly slow, and
Sam reckoned that it was becoming even
slower. When he caught an occasional
glimpse of the lights out at sea, they seemed
no closer. Push . . . kick . . . push. Keep
going, Sam said to himself, and don't think
about anything else.

They were still moving steadily forward
when Zack groaned. He lifted his head,
peered at Sam and Jo, who were swimming
side by side, guiding the raft, and seemed to

realize where he was. He yelled something and pushed himself to his knees, grabbing wildly at the raft under him.

'Keep still!' Jo shouted.

The raft tilted and Zack slid sideways, half into the water. Sam took hold of him. He began to kick and struggle and Sam thought he would never be able to hold him. Jo was hanging on to the other side of the plunging raft, trying to steady it, but it was not until Russ joined her, gasping at the pain of his injured hands, that they managed to get it level again.

Even then Sam couldn't haul Zack out of the water; he had lapsed into semi-consciousness again, he was moaning continuously, and he was almost a dead weight.

'This guy is getting to be a real pain,' Jo said through her teeth.

'He can't help it,' Sam said.

Mike came paddling round towards Sam, obviously meaning to help.

'Stay clear,' Sam warned him, terrified that Zack would revive and grab Mike.

Carefully Jo worked her way round the edge of the raft until she could get a grip on

Zack's shoulders and help Sam to drag him back until he lay on top of it again.

'If he's wrecked my camera, I'll kill him,' said Russ, trying to grin. 'Come on.'

He let go of the edge of the raft, and started to sink.

Mike, who was nearest, shoved his pumice float under Russ's arms; the man lay, half across it, coughing up water. The extra effort of manoeuvring the raft had taken almost all his remaining strength.

Sam fought for self-control. He couldn't just look on while his dad drowned. He had to do something. He gazed around him over the surface of the sea.

Here the floating pumice was more scattered, as if they were reaching its furthest edge. The light of the rescue boat was over to the left; Sam found it hard to judge how far away. Too far, he thought. We're not going to make it. Fury coursed through him. We've done all this, we're so close, but we're not going to make it.

Zack had lapsed into unconsciousness again. Russ was barely able to hold his head up, and without Mike's float he would have gone under. Mike had found himself another float, but he too looked exhausted.

Sam's eyes met Jo's.

'*They've* got to come to *us*,' she said.

'The flash.' Sam groped for his father's camera, still fastened to Zack's belt. After the battering it had been through and the soaking it had taken in the sea water, he would not have been surprised if it had refused to work – despite its waterproof case. But when he switched on the flash gun, he soon heard the soft whirr as it powered up and he breathed a sigh of relief. He raised it as high as he could and pressed the button.

The blue-white flash reflected off the water and then left them in total darkness again. For a minute, Sam touched the depths of despair. They hadn't seen.

Then he heard the sound of an engine starting up. The distant light of the rescue boat began to move.

'Yes!' yelled Jo.

The growl of the engine grew louder. Then a wave lifted the raft and Sam saw the boat, a sleek, dark shape, bearing down on them, with a bright searchlight mounted in its bows. Jo cheered and raised an arm to wave. Sam shouted, his voice hoarse from weariness.

The helmsman must have heard them. The boat changed course, and the searchlight swept across the waves until it picked out the little group clinging round the pumice raft.

'They've seen us!' Mike shouted. 'They're here!'

The boat cut its engines and the foaming water at its bows died away. Its speed slowed and it slid gently alongside the raft. Sam grabbed a ladder as it drew level with him and he blinked in the brightness of the searchlight.

Jo said, 'Zack can't climb, or your dad. I'll go up and tell them.'

She gripped the ladder and pulled herself up out of the water. Sam saw an arm reach down to help her as she left the circle of light.

'Mike, you go as well,' Sam ordered.

Mike grinned at him and hauled himself up the side of the boat.

Sam waited, steadying the raft, while his dad trod water; Russ looked totally exhausted now and was relying entirely on Mike's discarded float to buoy him up.

It seemed an eternity to Sam, but it couldn't have been more than a few minutes before one of the crew came down the ladder and fitted a harness round Russ to lift him to safety. Russ turned to Sam. 'Are you OK?'

'Fine, Dad. I'll see you on board.'

He watched Russ disappear upwards, and a little while later the harness came back for Zack. The crewman said in a strongly accented voice, 'Up you go, boy. I see to him.'

'I can wait,' said Sam.

He wasn't afraid that the crewman didn't know his job, but he felt that he had to see this through to the end; he had to be sure that all his party were accounted for. The crewman shrugged and didn't argue, and Sam held the raft in place while the man harnessed up the unconscious body of Zack and yelled out an order to lift him.

Then he gestured to Sam. 'Now you go.'

As Sam grabbed the first rung of the ladder, he turned back and said a silent goodbye to the pumice raft. They wouldn't be here now without it. Then he dragged himself upwards, still dazzled by the searchlight, until he could sprawl on the solid, welcoming boards of the deck.

Someone wrapped a blanket round him. Sam found that he was shivering violently. In the water he had never thought about being cold.

While Sam was recovering, some of the crew lifted Zack and carried him below decks. Russ paused to rest a hand on Sam's shoulder before he stumbled after them, clutching his camera protectively. Sam wondered if he ought to follow, but he couldn't resist glancing back for a last look at Tangaroa.

The whole island was silhouetted against a sky that still churned with smoke and fumes. Burning lava streaked the cone and streamed down the lower slopes, to form a frill of fiery gold near the shoreline. Glowing sparks and sluggish red smoke still spouted from the summit. Fire was reflected on the water, broken up by the dark shapes of the floating pumice.

Near by, Mike, huddled in his blanket, had curled up on the deck and was peering out between the railings of the boat. Jo was standing next to him; even though she must have been exhausted, she stood upright, her head thrown back. Sam gathered the folds of his blanket round himself and went to lean on the rail beside her.

'We did it,' she said. 'We really did it.'

Sam said nothing. He was still finding it hard to believe that they had made it to safety after all, and that the terror of their race down the mountainside would soon be no more than a memory. He was half afraid that standing on the deck of the rescue boat would turn out to be a dream, and that soon he would wake up and find himself surrounded by the encroaching lava.

But just then the boat's engine cut in. The boat began to move, slowly at first and then faster, sweeping round in a circle, away from the litter of pumice on the surface of the sea.

Sam looked back along the foaming wake, as Tangaroa fell away behind them. 'You know,' he said, 'I've just thought of something.'

'What?' asked Jo.

'Something Mum said this morning, before we left.' Was it only this morning? Sam found it hard to believe. 'She said that by the time we came back, all three of us would be friends.'

Jo grinned and folded her arms along the rail. 'Well, she was right about that, wasn't she?'

Sam looked back at the burning mountain and thought of the risks they had taken together and the teamwork that had brought them through. 'Yes,' he said. 'She certainly was.'

VOLCANOES

THE ESSENTIAL SURVIVAL GUIDE

Volcanoes create the greatest natural explosions in the world.

They're spectacular, but deadly, and can change the shape of landscapes for ever.

If a volcano erupted at full strength you could expect some or all of the following:

A continuous rain of smothering ash and super-heated mud

●

Furnace-hot winds that flatten and burn everything in their path

●

Fountains and rivers of molten lava

●

Clouds of choking, suffocating gases

●

Fiery rock bombs the size of cars

●

Dense clouds that can obscure the sun for weeks

●

Huge tidal waves (also known as tsunami) that can flatten coastal cities

●

Staggering, ear-splitting noise

VOLANOES DESTROY

Warnings

In recent years, satellites have been widely used to help detect imminent and increased volcanic activity around the world's hot spots. Satellite tracking systems can identify a build-up of the most common tell-tale gases and fluctuations in heat that may indicate an eruption is likely to occur.

Earth tremors or even earthquakes can also some-times herald a major volcanic eruption.

If a volcano was about to blow near you, warnings would be issued from the local Disaster Prevention Office on the radio, in newspapers, on TV and by official monitors patrolling the surrounding affected areas.

You would be told:

● when the eruption is expected
● which area is most likely to be affected
● what type of eruption to expect (see page 10)
● the timetable for evacuation procedures

In some countries, warnings are also given by the ringing of church bells.

Despite improved warning systems, most volcanoes remain unpredictable. Even those considered dormant for many years can unexpectedly become active again.

3

Evacuation!

If you lived close to an active volcano that was expected to erupt, you would have to be prepared to evacuate your home at short notice. You may have to travel on foot, by car or by truck or even by ship in coastal areas.

DO NOT argue with the authorities if you are told to leave your home. It is for your own safety. In most places you would face a fine if you were to enter a forbidden zone near an active volcano.

DO stay calm.

DO NOT guess where you need to go. The experts can predict with some accuracy which areas are most likely to be affected.

DO find out exactly where the safe havens are located. Emergency shelters are often set up in schools and community halls.

DO leave everything behind that you don't need.

DO NOT stay around to watch the spectacle. It may be an incredible sight, but the consequences are not worth the risk.

You could increase your chances of surviving a volcanic blast by wearing an Emergency

Escape Hood, which was developed by the US Navy. The hood is placed over your head and a tube connected to a canister of compressed air allows you to breathe. However, even this would keep you alive for no more than thirty minutes.

Poisonous, evil-smelling sulphurous volcanic gas and odourless carbon dioxide are more lethal than lava, pumice or ash. The ejected gas can remove all oxygenated air from a very large area in a matter of minutes.

Lava 'ash flows' or 'glowing avalanches' can speed down a volcano at up to 100 kmph and would be impossible to outrun, which is why it is so important to evacuate the area as soon as possible.

The Journey

● If you are travelling by car, be sure you have enough petrol. Take a spare can of petrol. It may already be scarce and you will need all the supplies you can obtain.

● Dust off any ash and debris that may have accumulated on your car if it has been left out in the open.

● Check the engine. Electric cables can easily be torn or burned through by ash and pumice.

● Take plenty of bottled water or other drinks to quench your thirst throughout your journey. The heat and dry air near a volcano will make you especially thirsty.

● During the journey, you may need to keep on the wipers to clear any ash falling on the windscreen. Close all windows to avoid a build up of ash dust.

● Beware of ash bowls – large holes in the road filled to surface level with ash. They may be more than a metre deep, and like quicksand in places.

● If your vehicle is stuck, leave it and make your way on foot.

Aftermath

Protect yourself
Stay fully dressed and try to protect all of your exposed skin. Wear shoes that cover your feet completely. They should have thick soles to stop your feet from being burnt if the ground is still hot.

You should wear a mask over your nose and mouth as you clear up to avoid breathing in fine dust. Brush yourself down regularly.

Conserve provisions
Little, if anything, will be available to buy locally after a volcanic eruption. It will take time for life to return to normal. Eat any stored foodstuffs sparingly – it may be a long time before the emergency services arrive to help out.

Don't be fooled!
Stay well clear of any slow-moving lava. Intense heat from the viscous, molten rock can cause flash fires all along its path and endanger many lives.

Mind your head
Do not re-enter your home unless you are told it is safe to do so. But once it is, clear loose ash from roofs and window sills. A build up of this type of heavy debris can cause structural damage. Ash-laden buildings and walls may be unstable.

Volcanoes – The Facts

What?
A volcano is a mountain or hill that contains one or more openings in the earth's crust through which lava, cinders, steam, gases and other matter are forcefully ejected – continuously or at intervals.

Where?
Volcanoes are likely to occur wherever one or more of the earth's continental plates meet. Most active is The Ring of Fire – roughly the area surrounding the Pacific Ocean. Major volcanoes are also found in the mid-Atlantic Ocean, in the West Indies, the Hawaiian islands, the Mediterranean and Indonesia.

When?
Volcanic activity is extremely unpredictable. Earth tremors, increased temperatures and minor eruptions can all indicate rising activity. However, even with modern technology, only rarely will sufficient warning be given to prepare fully for a major eruption.

Complex Volcano

Strato Volcano

How?

Volcanoes begin as hot spots – molten magma builds up in huge chambers deep underneath the earth's crust. Under great pressure, the magma begins to move towards the surface through fizzures. When the crust is eventually punctured, a volcanic eruption occurs and continues until the pressure underground subsides. Eruptions can also be triggered by the escape of gases or by the side of a volcano collapsing.

Effect?

It is believed that volcanoes have helped form a large part of the earth's physical geography over millions of years. These explosive eruptions are often spectacular, always extremely loud, and the materials a volcano throws out are usually deadly. Eruptions also affect the weather. Ash ejected into the sky can linger over a massive area and appear to blot out the sun for weeks.

Types of Volcano

Volcanoes come in a number of different shapes and sizes, some of which are illustrated below.

Somma Volcano   Caldera

Shield Volcano

Types of Volcanic Eruption

There are three main types of volcano – the Strombolian, the Vulcanian and the Pelean.

The strength of the explosion depends upon many factors – particularly the magma's gas content and its viscosity, which influences the way in which gas escapes the liquid.

Strombolian
This features intermittent, low-intensity explosions triggered by bubbles bursting in the magma.

Vulcanian
Vulcanian eruptions are more explosive. They feature the ejection of old, accumulated lava and matter by a build-up of gasses in the vent below.

Pelean
Pelean eruptions are the most destructive. Fine ash, super-heated steam and new fragmented magma are thrown out in a continual and colossal rolling, billowing mass.

Risk Zones

Areas are classified according to the level of risk when a volcanic eruption is imminent. Though these classifications vary slightly from country to country, the risk zones are:

Zone A: Most likely to be hit – closed to all but scientists.

Zone B: Closed to all but essential service people – who visit for short periods and must carry short-wave radio at all times.

Zone C: The 'safe' area for collection of evacuees.

Size does Matter!

The amount of ash (measured in cubic kilometres) that a volcano emits is often a good measure of the size of the eruption. The diagram on page 12 compares the emissions of five major eruptions.

Most of the major volcanic mountains in the world are over 3,000 metres high and the effect of their ejected debris can be substantial. For example, the Unzen volcano in Japan threw out enough pumice over a period of twenty years until 1800 that it was possible to walk twenty-three miles out to sea on the floating pumice.

The size of the rocks thrown out during an explosion can be enormous. The Asama volcano in Japan threw out blocks of rock up to thirteen metres in diameter.

11

The Santa Maria volcano in Guatamala threw out so much lava that it eventually stretched for 323,750 square metres, to a depth of twenty centimetres.

3km³ of ash

80km³ of ash

Vesuvius, Italy AD 79

Tambora, Indonesia 1815

18km³ of ash

12km³ of ash

1km³ of ash

St Helens, USA 1980

Volcanoes
– The Biggies

Place: Mount Vesuvius, Naples, Italy

Date: AD 79

Death toll: At least 3,500

Effect: Vesuvius had been dormant for centuries by Roman times, so the area around the volcano and the nearby Bay of Naples was densely populated. On the afternoon of 24 August the volcano suddenly came back to life. A tremendous roaring sound filled the air as a huge trail of ash was blown into the sky. The volcano became increasingly active. After showers of pumice and stones, the west rim of the volcano was blown away in a massive explosion that was seen for many miles. Most of those living in the nearby cities of Pompeii and Herculaneum were killed outright. The eruption was recorded by a young scholar of the time called Pliny the Younger. His descriptive letters to Tacitus are the first known eyewitness accounts of a volcanic eruption.

13

Place: Mount Etna, Sicily
Date: 1669
Death toll: 100,000 approx.
Effect: When Mount Etna blew spectacularly in the late seventeenth century, the sun appeared to be blotted out for months. A second explosion created a crack in the side of the mountain nineteen kilometres long and two metres wide. Six further craters also erupted. Red-hot stone, sand and ash were thrown from these craters over 233 square kilometres. Then the great central crater split, spilling out a huge mass of lava. Fifty towns were buried by the flow. Exact statistics about the probable death toll are unknown – except that it was massive.

Place: Tambora, Indonesia
Date: 1815
Death toll: 92,000 appox.
Effect: This was probably the most spectacular explosion in recent history. Tambora was a 4,000 metre-high mountain. It erupted with such force that the island on which it stood, sank. As it went down, 1.7 million tonnes of rubble were blown into the sky. The explosion caused the 'year without a summer' as the sun was blotted out by the resulting dust. It was so cold that washing hung out during the day in Plymouth, Connecticut, USA sometimes froze! Most of the loss of life was due to starvation in the subsequent weeks and months following the eruption.

14

Place: Krakatau, Indonesia
Date: 1883
Death toll: 200,000 approx.
Effect: The island of
Krakatau (or Krakatoa)
began to erupt in May
1883, throwing huge
amounts of dust into the sky.
By late-August the explosions
became more threatening. During the
night of 26 and 27 August, the island was blown
apart. It then disappeared in a massive explosion –
one of the loudest ever – that was heard 4,000 kilometres away at Alice Springs in Australia. Debris
climbed into the air and the sky turned black. The
resultant shock waves were so great that they travelled around the world seven times and created a
huge wall of water, over thirty metres high, which
destroyed hundreds of coastal communities.
Floating islands of pumice drifted across the Indian
Ocean for several months afterwards causing a
great hazard to ships.

Place: Mount Katmai, Alaska
Date: 1912
Death toll: Zero
Effect: In this unpopulated
area, the Katmai volcano
erupted with such terrific force
that the explosion, ash and
debris turned the local green,
wooded valleys into an eighty

15

kilometre square area of devastation. It is the biggest volcanic eruption in America in recorded history. Numerous smoking fumeroles were left by the volcano and the area became known as the Valley of 10,000 Smokes. It remained so lifeless a region that it served as a training ground for the astronauts going to the moon.

Place: Mount St Helen's, Washington State, USA
Date: 1980
Death toll: 62
Effect: For 123 years the modestly sized Mount St Helen's was dormant. Then, on 20 March 1980, a series of earth tremors shook the area as the volcano signalled its intention to reawaken. For two months the shape of the volcano changed as magma began to bulge beneath the cone. The bulge slowly crept across an area of two miles. By 18 May the bulge had become so steep and weak that it collapsed and caused the world's largest recorded landslide. Gas erupted from the hole and caused an unexpected and lethal sideways blast. Ash and massive mud flows followed. The whole area was devastated. Day turned to night. So much ash was blown into the upper atmosphere that it circled the world for eleven days. The eruption caused $3 billions' worth of damage.

Ten of the greatest volcanic eruptions of all time

Krakatau, Indonesia
26–28 August 1883   200,000 dead

Mount Etna, Sicily
11 March 1669   60–100,000 dead

Tambora, Indonesia
5–12 April 1815   92,000 dead

Unzen, Japan
1 April 1793   53,000 dead

Santorini, Greece
August 1470 BC   50,000 dead

Mount Pelée, Martinique
8 May 1902   36,000 dead

Nevada del Ruiz, Colombia
14–16 November 1985   25,000+ dead

Laki, Iceland
January–June 1783   9,000+ dead

Kelut, Indonesia
December 1919   5,500 dead

Mount Mayon, Philippines
1 February 1815   2,200+ dead

Volcanic jargon

Ash
Fine fragments of rock thrown out by a volcanic eruption.

Caldera
The basin-like crater at the top of a volcano left after an explosion or eruption.

Cinder cones
Steep, but small, volcanoes, that often erupt with great force.

Eruption cloud
The columns of gas, rocks and ash that can explode from a volcano.

Fissure
A crack in the ground through which lava will flow. When molten rock comes out it is called a fissure eruption.

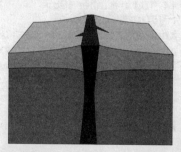

Lahar
A highly destructive mud flow, formed where lava or ash meets snow, ice or water.

Lava
Molten rock spewed from volcanoes or vents in the earth. Fountains of liquid lava can reach 120 metres in the air and flow at up to two metres an hour. Its weight is such that little can actually stop it – even bombs have been used to try and divert it – but failed. The longest lava flow in history, in Iceland in 1783, covered ninety-five square kilometres.

Magma
Molten rock within the earth that is called lava if it is erupted.

Pumice
Lightweight volcanic rock full of gas bubbles thrown from an eruption.

Pyroclastic flow
The name for the flow of solid or semi-solid material, including lumps of rock thrown out during a volcanic eruption.

Volcanologist
A scientist who studies volcanoes.

Weird!

The volcanic mud at Pompeii and Herculaneum, near Mount Vesuvius, perfectly preserved the bodies of the people and animals in both towns after the eruption in AD 79!

Dust from the explosion of Krakatau in 1883 travelled round the world for several months producing spectacular coloured sunsets in Europe, where the moon and the sun appeared blue or green.

One of only two people left alive in the town of St Pierre on the French Caribbean island of Martinique when Mount Pelée erupted in 1902 was a prisoner condemned to death. Auguste Ciparis survived because his cell had thick walls with one tiny window that faced away from the volcano. He was later pardoned!

The Mexican Mount Paricutin volcano of 1943 was 'the volcano that grew in a cornfield'. From nothing, it reached 365 metres in seven months. It had begun as a hole in the ground fifty years before!